PRAISE FOR

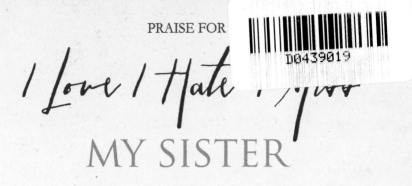

MY SISTER

An Amelia Bloomer Project List Selection
A CBC Notable Social Studies Trade Book of the Year
A Bank Street Best Book of the Year with Outstanding Merit
An NYC Reads 365 Selection

"Thought-provoking." —*Kirkus Reviews*

"Important and timely." —*Booklist*

"Sarn's poignant novel surely raises issues of religious freedom, but it is foremost a coming-of-age story about personal choice and the uniquely powerful bond between sisters." —*The Horn Book Magazine*

"[A] moving story, which provides rich material for conversation about family relations, religious identity, and civil liberties." —*Publishers Weekly*

"In seamless chapters transitioning between present and past, this [is a] short, fast-paced, tragic story contrasting two clearly drawn Muslim sisters." —*School Library Journal*

"A fair and balanced look at not just two equal and opposite perspectives on these issues, but at the multiple, refracted, messy nuances in between." —*The Bulletin*

"A searing portrait of the conflicts within a culture." —*VOYA*

"Sarn writes with concise, timely insight about culture, religion, and politics, but what lingers most is the powerful bonds of sisterhood." —smithsonianapa.org

I Love I Hate I Miss

MY SISTER

Amélie Sarn

Translated from the French
by Y. Maudet

EMBER

Translation copyright © 2014 by Y. Maudet
Cover photograph copyright © 2014 by Emrah Altinok/Getty Images
Interior art copyright © 2014 by Shutterstock

All rights reserved. Published in the United States by Ember, an imprint of Random House
Children's Books, a division of Penguin Random House LLC, New York. The English
translation was first published in hardcover by Delacorte Press, an imprint of Random
House Children's Books, a division of Penguin Random House LLC, in 2014. Originally
published in paperback in France as *Un Foulard Pour Djelila* by Éditions Milan, Paris, in
2005. Original French text copyright © 2005 by Éditions Milan. Updated French text and
illustration copyright © 2008 by Éditions Milan.

Ember and the E colophon are registered trademarks of Penguin Random House LLC.

Visit us on the Web! randomhouseteens.com

Educators and librarians, for a variety of teaching tools, visit us at RHTeachersLibrarians.com

The Library of Congress has cataloged the hardcover edition of this work as follows:
Sarn, Amélie.
[Foulard pour Djelila. English]
I love I hate I miss my sister / Amélie Sarn ;
translated from the French by Y. Maudet. — First American edition.
pages cm
"Originally published in France as *Un Foulard Pour Djelila* by Éditions Milan, Paris, in
2005"—Copyright page.
Summary: "Portrait of two Muslim sisters, once closely bonded, but now on divergent paths
as one embraces her religion and the other remains secular"—Provided by publisher.
ISBN 978-0-385-74376-1 (hardback) — ISBN 978-0-375-99128-8 (glb) —
ISBN 978-0-385-37020-2 (ebook) [1. Sisters—Fiction. 2. Muslims—Fiction.
3. Death—Fiction.] I. Maudet, Y., translator. II. Title.
PZ7.S24828Iam 2014
[Fic]—dc23
2014005094

ISBN 978-0-385-74377-8 (trade pbk.)

Printed in the United States of America

10 9 8 7 6 5 4 3 2 1

First Ember Edition 2016

ACKNOWLEDGMENTS

My thanks to everyone who so graciously accepted to answer my questions on various aspects of the Muslim religion of which I was ignorant—especially Mohammadi and her sisters, and Maud, who was my enlightened go-between as well as advisor on various other points.

I Love I Hate I Miss

MY SISTER

The women walk slowly, heads down. They hold a banner that stretches across the length of the street.

WE HAVE NOT FORGOTTEN YOU, DJELILA!

As they make their way through the Lilac housing projects, followed by parents, friends, and strangers, some who were watching from their windows come down to join the silent procession. Maybe they *had* forgotten.

The group stops in front of the tower where Djelila lived, the tower where her parents, her brothers, Idriss and Taïeb, and her sister, Sohane, live still.

But this morning Sohane isn't home. She's at the foot of the tower, bare-headed; she helps carry the banner.

Flowers have been placed on the stone slab embedded in

the ground like a tombstone. The slab commemorates the tragedy of that day, a year ago. Exactly a year ago.

The slab where slurs have been tagged and erased three times this year. Three times in just one year.

Sohane's eyes fill with tears.

This morning she did not cover her head. It would have been useless. It is her whole face she wants to hide.

2

One

"Sohane, can I borrow your jeans?"

"No, I already told you, Djelila."

I don't feel like lending Djelila my jeans again. Not that I want to wear them, because I don't. Ever since the last time Djelila borrowed them and I saw how much better they fit her, I no longer feel like wearing them.

"Come on, little sis, please."

"No. And I'm not your little sis. I'm a year older than you, remember?"

"Sohane . . ."

I roll my eyes. Djelila isn't giving up. I know she'll soon come and sit beside me, ask me what I'm reading, get up to tell me all about the incredible shot she made from the middle of the basketball court in one of her dreams last night. She'll pretend to focus, bend her knees, throw an imaginary ball, put on a dazed look as she explains that the ball is rolling around the rim of the basket; then she'll burst out with a whoop when, at last, it falls in, adding the three points needed for the win.

"The referee whistles the end of the game!" she'll shout. "And the crowd stomps onto the court and lifts me up on their shoulders. Coach Abdellatif congratulates me and declares that I am the best player of all time; the college recruiters are here to watch me. . . ."

And she will manage to make me laugh.

My sister is beautiful.

Very beautiful.

Djelila has fine features, soft and silky skin, not one spot of acne. She is tall, her smile and her dark eyes radiant. She's wearing only a T-shirt, a pair of shorts, and high-tops. Her thighs are long and muscular, her legs, as always, perfectly smooth.

Lending her my jeans is out of the question.

"Tell me, Sohane, what do you think of Jeremy?" she asks.

Just as I predicted, Djelila comes to sit beside me. We've always shared a bedroom. All of my memories include her. I love no one else more than my little sister and I hate no one else as much.

"Who's Jeremy?"

"The guy in twelfth grade."

"Oh, him. Well . . ."

4

"Is that all you have to say? He's as handsome as a god."

"Don't talk that way, Djelila. You know I don't like it."

Djelila laughs. "Sorry, he's killer handsome. Is that better?"

I would rather not answer. Djelila talks the way she wants to; that's her problem. But I don't have to listen to her using the word "god" so casually.

"Don't give me that disapproving look," Djelila says, smiling as she scoots closer. "Tell me what you think of Jeremy."

I put down my book on the night table that separates our beds. The room is small.

"Why do you ask? Does he want to go out with you?"

Djelila shakes her head. "I noticed him at the gym the other day, after practice," she says. "I think he's on the handball team. I couldn't stop staring at him, but he didn't even look at me."

"And that's what's bothering you?"

"No. I like him. That's all."

"You don't even know him."

"Well, I like him anyway."

"You're going to get into trouble again, Djelila."

Racine High School is on the outskirts of our housing project. It's a large complex composed of five buildings swarming with 2,153 students, grades eleven through twelve, plus three vocational divisions. I'm in twelfth grade; Djelila is in eleventh. At school, we go unnoticed. It's as if we lead another life. As if we have multiple personalities—

one for our parents, a second for the projects, and a third for high school.

Unfortunately, the partitions are sometimes fragile.

Djelila already learned this the hard way.

"Do you mean Majid and his gang?" Djelila says. "Whatever. I'm not afraid of them! They're a bunch of losers with nothing better to do than sit on the project benches and spy on us. They're jealous, that's all. Because we're happy!"

I am not going to remind her that two days ago I found her crying in front of the elevator. Her mascara had run around her eyes. I'm the one who told her to calm down, not to let those lowlifes get to her, just to let them spit their venom. "Ignore them, that's the best thing you can do," I said.

In the elevator, Djelila put her head on my shoulder and I wiped off her mascara with a tissue. She whispered, "Thank you." When we entered our apartment, she went directly to the bathroom to clean her face, then came out and joined Mom in the kitchen; I went to our room to do my homework. From there, I could hear the two of them laughing.

Dad's voice intrudes on my thoughts.

"Girls, dinner's ready," he says.

He knocks on the door and walks off. He never comes into our room. He would never even think of opening the door. As if he's afraid of what he might see. This amuses Djelila. On purpose, she'll ask our mother, right in front of him, if she has seen these underpants or that bra. "You know, the pink one with double straps? I can't find it," Djelila will say. She thinks it's fun to see Dad stiffen over his newspaper, pretending that he doesn't hear a thing.

"A girl's space must stay a girl's space," he explains to our little brother Taïeb, who listens wide-eyed. "Women have secrets that we don't need to know about. We must respect their privacy."

Taïeb doesn't understand. All he wants is to barge into our room and play with us. Actually, because Dad forbids it, it allows us to have some peace.

A slip of paper is shoved under our door. Someone scribbled on it with a purple felt marker: *Dinner is reddy*. It's Idriss's handwriting. He's in first grade, a few years younger than Taïeb, and spends all his time writing even though he hasn't started to learn spelling yet.

I push Djelila away and get up.

"Come on, let's go have dinner," I say.

Djelila rises, smiling, kisses my cheek for no good reason, and puts on her old pajama pants, the same ones she has worn for at least two years. Softly she walks toward the door, laughing.

She is beautiful, my sister.

I envy how she is so carefree.

Two

"Carefree." What a strange word.

My parents refused to move out.

Dad refused because he can't bear to leave Djelila. Mom has no opinion. She's in denial. She refuses to believe what happened.

Taïeb and Idriss have grown. Aunt Algia had her baby—a girl she named after her mother, Hebtissem. It's strange that time does not stop.

I feel like running away. Final exams are at the end of the school year. I will ace them and get my diploma. Then I will leave. So I work hard, losing myself in my books. I'm oblivious to the difference between night and day. For me, the world is a small, narrow bedroom with twin beds and two desks—a space terrifying and comforting at the same time.

Three

"Sohane, wait for me."

"Hurry up, then!"

Djelila hoists her bags over her shoulders—one filled with schoolbooks, the other stuffed with her basketball gear—shoves a slice of bread into her mouth, and takes the stairs four at a time behind me.

"We're always late because of you," I complain as we head outside.

"Why are you always in such a hurry to get to school?"

Djelila throws what's left of her bread into the square. *Bon appétit*, birds.

My sister never has time for a proper breakfast. But there is no way she would go to school without doing her hair just so and carefully applying makeup. Not too much, just a light trace of powder to hide a tiny blemish on her chin, mascara, and some kohl to line her eyes. Only what's needed.

At the bus stop, a woman wearing a djellaba is waiting, a shopping bag in her hand. I glance at her, then at the ads on the bus shelter. One ad shows a girl wearing nothing more than a G-string, her buttocks on full view. The full-size ad is supersexy. You can't see the model's face, which makes you think she has no face. She's only a pair of butt cheeks. I am disgusted by this display of flesh. I look at my sister. Makeup isn't the only weapon in her feminine arsenal. She's wearing jeans that hug her curves, a close-fitting sweater so short it exposes her back when she bends down, and a mini-hoodie. She is lovely. So superficial. It's probably her age. I'm only eleven months older than Djelila, but I don't feel the need to expose parts of my body. My sweaters are long enough to cover my waist. And even if I don't feel like lending my tight jeans to Djelila, I don't wear them anymore. I've switched to a pair of looser-fitting cotton pants. They may not be as stylish as jeans, but they're more comfortable.

Besides, I don't want a boy to look at me because he's attracted to my bared skin. I want something more. Something better.

Conceit is a sin. I know.

School isn't so far that we can't walk, but in the morning the bus gives us time to relax and prepare ourselves for the change in atmosphere.

The bus pulls up in front of the stop. It's almost empty.

We're at the beginning of the line. It will be full by the time we reach school. Djelila and I sit side by side, always in the same seats, in the first row at the middle of the bus. We put our bags on the floor and prop our knees up against the glass partition. We are still sisters for a few more stops. After that, we part ways—as if we've crossed an invisible border. The projects border.

Beyond that limit, my sister changes. She sits back a little more and puts her feet on her bag. The Djelila of the Lilac housing projects becomes the Djelila of Racine High School. One stop farther and Karine and Estelle join us. Djelila gets up and holds on to the pole to be closer to her friends. They talk about their teachers, about some of their classmates, about the last math lesson, which none of them understood. I wonder if Karine and Estelle even know that Djelila and I are sisters. If they do, they couldn't care less.

When we get off the bus, the crowd separates us. We don't bother to look at each other. Djelila no longer knows me.

I walk toward my friends, if you can call them that. They're just the students from class who I get along with: Lola, Sofia, Christian, and Charlene. They are huddled near the main door, smoking. I do not smoke. I am Muslim. My parents taught me that we have to respect the body that God gave us.

Djelila goes her own way. Up until last week, Sylvan, a boy who's also a junior but in another class, greeted my sister with a kiss. Hand in hand they would join their friends.

They made a cute couple. It lasted a month and a half. A short-lived love story. Djelila filled me in on the details at night, when the light was out. Ever since she started flirting in tenth grade, she's told me everything. She had never gone out with a boy for such a long time, but she broke it off last week because she got fed up. "Sylvan's too dull" is what she told me. My sister needs passion. Sylvan looked unhappy for a few days, but now he seems better. He still hangs out with Djelila and the others, and yesterday I saw them all laughing together.

I've never gone out with a boy. Djelila sometimes makes fun of me, in a nice way. She claims that Basil, the tall blond guy in her class, is crazy about me; she says I have a long list of admirers and that my indifference will drive them to suicide. She swears that a little bit of kohl would bring out the beauty of my eyes, that I'm very pretty when I smile. Of course, hearing her say these things makes me smile.

Djelila just lit a cigarette. Dad would not like that.

Four

Dad would not have liked it.

"I thought you were an athlete," I told Djelila.

"Yeah, so what?"

"Well, since when does nicotine boost endurance and the ability to shoot a basket from the mid-court?"

"Give it up, Sohane. What's it to you if I smoke?"

"Nothing. It's your problem. I'm just saying that for such a serious basketball player you—"

"I barely smoke one cigarette a day."

I was using the sports argument, but Djelila wasn't buying it. We had already discussed the subject. Long before, Mom—at Dad's request—asked Djelila why she no longer went to the mosque.

Mom made no demands. She just wanted to know

the reason. Djelila mumbled some answer; she knew our parents worried about her. After all, if you don't go to the mosque, and if you stop praying, you're condemned to hell. Djelila explained to Mom that she didn't really have time anymore, what with homework and basketball. . . . "But I pray, Mom, I recite all my prayers," she lied to her.

Mom turned to me for confirmation and I nodded and said, "Yes, Mom, we pray together." This was a lie too, but it reassured Mom, who in turn eagerly reassured Dad.

I tried to delve deeper into the question.

"Don't you believe in God anymore, Djelila?" I asked.

You shrugged. "I don't know. I don't think about it. I don't feel like thinking about it."

Of course you didn't feel like thinking about it.

You inhaled your cigarette smoke with relish that morning and started to cough. Karine slapped your back and you burst out laughing. You couldn't stop. You laughed like crazy, like the crazy pretty girl you were.

I thought you smoked to prove yourself, to appear self-confident. I was right, probably. But I couldn't understand why you wanted so badly to belong to that group. They were all so ordinary. All they cared about was their looks, their love lives, the movies they went to see. I saw it as a betrayal, a way for you to detach yourself from us, a way to reject and repudiate us. I told you as much sometimes: "You're different when you're at school, Djelila, you're not the same. You play a part. Why?"

You always answered fiercely: "You too, Sohane, you're different at school."

You were right.

You added that it was at school that you felt like yourself. That when you were with your friends you didn't feel the need to pretend to be someone you weren't. You could laugh loudly, smoke, and talk without having to watch what you said. You felt free.

I didn't believe you.

"All you want is to be like everyone else. To disappear in the crowd," I accused you. "But you're better than that!"

"Really? Better than that? Are you saying I should be like you? Is that what you mean?"

Irritated by what I considered your bad faith, I shrugged and went back to my books and my homework. I no longer understood you. What had happened to you?

Djelila, why are you no longer here? I want to hug you so badly.

Five

Five o'clock. In clusters, students come out of school. I'm in a hurry to get home. I have an essay to prepare. I feel more pressure than usual, with final exams almost here. The teachers do nothing to alleviate the stress. They only make it worse.

At midnight, I'm still working when Djelila brings me a glass of milk and some chocolate cookies.

"Your essay is going to be fine," she says as she looks over my notes. "You always explain what you want to say clearly. Not like me. Whenever I try, everything gets jumbled. . . ."

I don't answer. She goes on: "You should stop working now. You've done enough, don't you think?" I tell her that I can't sleep anyway. "Stress? You should relax, Sohane. Seriously. You'll be beat tomorrow. I'm going to bed." These few words that we exchange don't seem like much, and yet I drink my milk and I'm finally willing to go to bed. For the span of one night, I forget my classwork, teachers, and the looming exams that are like a monstrous dragon about to swallow me whole.

I spot Djelila and her friends in front of the school gate. They are saying goodbye to each other. Djelila is laughing, her white teeth gleaming. A boy bends toward her and whispers a few words in her ear. I don't know him. She pushes him back gently. He shrugs and blows her a kiss from his fingertips. Djelila shakes her head and walks off. My eyes stay glued on her. She has not seen them.

They've never come so close to school.

At least, I've never noticed them before—Majid, Youssef, Brahim, Mohad, Saïd—the gang from the projects. They are leaning against the school wall, "warming up the asphalt," as they like to say. It's their main pastime. But they're not here by accident. They don't seem to be looking in our direction, but I'm sure nothing that happened between Djelila and the boy escaped their notice.

Recently, my French teacher, Ms. Lombard, brought in an article about the rule of the Taliban in Afghanistan. A present-day medieval regime.

Ms. Lombard made it clear that the article wasn't related to our literature curriculum, which it definitely wasn't. But we read the article in class anyway.

It talked about the "Taliban police of vice and virtue" that patrolled the streets of Kabul. A bunch of bearded men who made it their job to ensure that, underneath their burkas, women weren't wearing any makeup, that their socks covered their ankles, maybe even made sure that their smiles did not offend God. The article made for a passionate discussion in class. It was a discussion, not a debate, since everyone was in agreement. The girls were shocked, and some boys made crude jokes. I didn't say anything; I just listened.

Now, at this very moment, I realize that *our* Taliban has arrived. They aren't bearded. Not yet. We're roughly the same age and even attended the same school before they dropped out. We played and learned to read together. Usually they stay within the housing project, their hands stuffed in the front pocket of their hoodies, shoulders hunched. Every day they become surer of themselves and assert themselves more and more, our little judges.

Of course, I'm not the one they're watching out of the corners of their eyes. It is Djelila who's got their attention. The too-beautiful Djelila.

It's difficult to notice anyone else.

She moves with a long elastic stride, her carefree attitude seemingly slung over her shoulders.

"Carefree." What a strange word.

She recently highlighted a strand of her hair with the help of hydrogen peroxide. I didn't try to talk her out of it.

It's not ugly. It's like a ray of sunshine in her dark brown hair.

Dad frowned when he saw it. He didn't say anything to his darling daughter, though—the treasure and apple of his eye, the amazing girl with gazelle eyes. He went straight to Mom. "Why did Djelila do that to her hair?" he grumbled. "Why does she want to transform herself? She's beautiful as she is. Why does she always need to be different? Haven't we given her enough?"

Mom shrugged. "Yes, your daughter is beautiful. And she's still beautiful, regardless of what she did. Give her a break."

Poor Dad! He shuffled off to the living room, mumbling some coarse words in Arabic—the few coarse words he knows. Then he shook his head and went back to his newspaper. That was the end of the incident.

Djelila walks fast. She doesn't want to be late for basketball practice. She crosses the lawn that separates the school from the gym, making sure not to step on any dog poop, and opens a door. She disappears inside.

I watch Majid and his gang. They huddle in discussion. I can't help thinking that with their hint of facial hair, and with the acne that is starting to eat up their cheeks, they have become ugly. What are they plotting? I see them head toward the gym. Although I have to work on my essay, I follow them.

The gym is ice-cold. The practice is under way. Djelila is focused on her shots. Her thrust is great. Each ball arcs in a perfect curve and falls right into the middle of the basket, hardly touching the rim. Coach Abdellatif blows a whistle and the team gathers quickly in front of him. Abdellatif is charismatic and kind and has a soft yet strong voice that enables him to get the best out of his team. He is tall, really good-looking, with long hair he keeps tied in a ponytail. Djelila says he's old—at thirty—but I'm sure she isn't indifferent to his charm. Personally, I think he's gorgeous.

Majid, Youssef, Brahim, Mohad, and Saïd are sitting in the bleachers. They are quiet, which I don't understand. I remain near the door, a strategic spot where no one can see me, and where I can make a quick getaway.

What are they waiting for? Do they think their presence will make Djelila lose her concentration? If that's the case, they're going to be sorely disappointed, because she hasn't even noticed them.

These five guys have been hanging out together for a few months now. In the projects, you can always find them in front of Tower 38, which they've clumsily tagged in red letters: THIS IS OUR PLACE. What a stupid and childish way to mark their territory.

"Just like dogs that pee along the walls," Djelila said, laughing, when she saw the tag.

Everyone considers them harmless in spite of their efforts to look tough. But it's true that they've become more confident and are quick to insult the girls who walk past Tower 38. *Their* tower. A barrage of insults fly out of their mouths: "whore," "bitch," "slut." They are so pathetic that nobody pays much attention to them. "At least they don't drink," Mom says sometimes.

Coach Abdellatif has organized a mini-game. The girls are sweating. Djelila seems to be everywhere on the court. She braided her long hair so it doesn't get in the way. She runs, snatches the ball from an opponent, dribbles, makes a pass, and races to the end of the court like a bolt of lightning. I haven't seen her play in a long time. She is astonishing.

The five dimwits talk quietly. Then Saïd spits on the floor with disgust.

Coach Abdellatif whistles to signal the end of the game. "You did great, girls! You fought like warriors! If you play like this next Saturday, you'll crush Montilan's team."

The girls whoop with joy. Abdellatif smiles before telling them to go change.

"Go on, get out of here, ladies!"

The girls swarm to the locker room like bees. Alice, one of the girls' team members, puts her arm around my sister's shoulders.

On the bleachers, the dimwits get up. I leave quickly, before they spot me.

I feel stupid. I'm hiding out along the side of the gym like a spy in a James Bond movie. Majid and his four loser friends appear and sit on a bench.

They look impassive and determined. As if they have a mission to accomplish.

The girls come out, Djelila first. Dad agreed to let her take part in basketball practice on the condition that she not come home too late. Djelila follows the rule. She waves goodbye to her friends, adjusts her bags on her shoulders, and starts walking home. She glances at Majid and his gang, rolls her eyes mockingly, and heads toward the projects.

They give her a head start before following her.

It's a strange procession: Djelila in front, the dimwits a few yards behind, and me, stuck to them all like a magnet.

As if I want to know what is going to happen.

As if I want to see what is going to happen.

We reach the housing projects.

Tower 38 is at the center.

Six

It's true that I let Djelila bleach her hair.

I think I was hoping the peroxide would burn it. I imagined the wavy strands hanging limply on each side of my sister's face.

The beautiful Djelila would no longer have been so beautiful.

Djelila, the treasure. Djelila with the gazelle eyes. These were the nicknames my father used when she was little. He has not forgotten them.

Last night, just before midnight, I left my room, left my lair. I wanted a glass of milk. Mom was already in bed. She's been sleeping a lot lately. It's her way of escaping.

Dad had fallen asleep in front of the TV. The screen cast a dull glow over him, over his cheeks covered in white twelve-o'clock shadow; on the screen, people were having a surreal dialogue and kissing.

Dad probably felt my presence. He didn't wake up, but he got agitated. I bent over him. He is old now.

I heard him mumble: "Djelila, my treasure. My gazelle-eyed Djelila."

Or am I the one who transformed the sound of his grinding teeth into tender words?

I went back to my room. I no longer wanted milk. I just wanted to work hard, so hard that I would have a way out of this place.

Seven

Djelila looks back. She senses them behind her, lying in wait for their prey. With courage, she sticks out her tongue at them and walks on.

They don't give up. They keep following her, at a quicker pace now, seemingly more determined. They are sure of themselves: the projects are their turf. In no time, they'll catch up to her.

I walk faster too. I don't know why. I don't know what I'm expecting, exactly.

The first insult is hurled. It comes from Majid. He used to be in love with Djelila when they were in preschool.

"Hey there, slut!"

My sister doesn't react. She keeps walking steadily, her back straight, the heels of her Nikes planted decidedly forward in the ground. But I know her well, and I'm sure she'll start to flinch soon. I'm sure her face already betrays fear.

"Little tramp!" Youssef says as he catches her arm. Djelila frees herself from his grip, but she's surrounded, with no way to flee.

"You're very stuck-up today."

"And for no good reason."

Brahim touches her hair, grabs a strand and releases it, then raises his hand as if he's going to slap her face. Djelila recoils reflexively, like a frightened gazelle.

Youssef laughs. "Are you afraid of us?" he yells. "You weren't afraid of boys when school let out. You know that you shame your religion, don't you?"

"Leave me alone."

It is not a shout, only a moan.

"You shame your religion, your family, and the whole projects!" Majid spits out. "We don't want girls like you around here. You're just a whore!"

"See how she dresses? How dare you go out of the projects looking like that! People are going to start saying that this place is full of prostitutes!" Mohad scowls. "Why not go naked while you're at it? All we see are your boobs and ass. Do you think that's dignified? Do you?"

"And what were you doing with that guy when you came out of school?" Saïd joins in. "You let him touch you. Filthy bitch! I swear, you make us cringe with shame!"

"And the way you jiggle up and down the gym. It's got to stop. Girls aren't meant to play sports!" Majid yells.

"Enough! Mind your own business!" Djelila shouts, getting her voice back. "I didn't ask your opinion!" She pushes Majid away from her. "And you, Hamzaoui Majid, who do you think you are? Have you forgotten that you were still wetting your pants in preschool? That you followed me around like a puppy? And now that you've got three hairs on your chin, you think you're a know-it-all? You think it's *Muslim* to judge me?"

My sister can fight back. The gazelle can become a lion. But she won't get out of this fix so easily. She should have kept her mouth shut. She should have apologized. She should have run off. A loud slap lands on her cheek. She didn't see it coming and didn't have time to protect herself.

Pleased with himself, Majid spits on the ground. "Women!" he says. "They don't show any respect today."

"But we're going to teach them! They're going to learn!"

"So you'd better dress properly. We don't want whores around here!"

"Yeah! Got it, slut?"

They all spit at Djelila's feet, and without another glance at her, they take off.

Djelila touches her cheek, her burning cheek. She lets her bags fall heavily to the ground. I decide that it's a good time to approach her.

"Djelila, what happened?" I ask, running toward her.

"It's . . . it's . . ."

Huge tears start streaming down her cheeks; her kohl starts running. Not too much: she hasn't rubbed her eyes

31

yet. She's still in shock. I hug her gently and she doesn't push me away.

"What happened? Did they call you names again?"

"They slapped me."

She is not sobbing. She just states a simple fact.

"It's Majid."

"Come, Djelila, let's keep moving."

I take hold of my sister's bags and pull her toward our building. She doesn't say a word. She steps into the elevator. She doesn't lean on my shoulder this time. The door opens. I hold her by the waist to support her, but she doesn't seem about to faint. I get the key out of my pocket even though I could have rung the bell. I can hear Mom inside with the little ones. I open the door.

A warm fragrance of freshly baked pastries fills the apartment.

"Is that you, girls?"

"Yes, Mom."

"Look at my drawing."

Taïeb, with his little face and his rosy cheeks, comes running out of the kitchen and holds out a sheet of paper on which he's painted a huge dinosaur.

"I did it at school."

Djelila gets hold of it before I do. She smiles at Taïeb and bends down to pick him up. Taïeb buries his nose in her neck.

"You smell good."

"Djelila!"

She turns her beautiful eyes toward me. "Thank you for being there, Sohane. Thank you," she says.

I bite my lips. "I'll put your bags in our room."

Djelila walks into the kitchen with Taïeb perched on her hip.

"You made gazelle horns, Mom!" she exclaims joyously. "Super!"

"Don't touch them, dear. They're for tonight."

"Do we have company coming?"

"Yes," Idriss says. "Uncle Ahmed and Aunt Algia. We'll get to stay up late."

"No way, kids. You'll be in bed by ten," Mom tells them.

"It's not fair," Idriss complains.

"What about Hana Leïla?" Djelila asks.

"Your grandmother isn't coming. She's still mad at Uncle Ahmed."

"Too bad, she's so funny."

I listen to this conversation from the corridor, my arms hanging at my sides. I decide to put the bags in our room and join Mom, my sister, and my brothers in the kitchen. Never mind the essay. I, too, want to listen to Mom's gentle voice and smell the vanilla-scented gazelle horns.

Eight

At the time, I thought, *Djelila will get what she deserves.*

It's not as if she had no warning. They had already insulted her once before. Still, she continued to provoke them.

Yes, this is what I thought, Djelila, my too-pretty little sister. Deep down, I wished they would teach you a lesson. That you would be knocked down a peg. That you wouldn't be so sure of yourself. That you would need me again, just like when we were little girls. Do you remember, Djelila? You and I, when we played together? I was the one in charge, the one who decided what adventure we would go on, the one who saved your life. I was also the one you wouldn't venture outside without, the one who held your hand to cross the streets, the one who read you stories, the one who comforted you when a boy bothered you at school.

35

You were a little girl whose big eyes turned to me whenever you were in doubt. I never resented Dad for calling you his treasure, because you were my treasure too. You always had more friends than I did. You loved to play and laugh. Do you remember the jump rope Uncle Ahmed bought for us? I could barely count to ten before getting all tangled up in it. But you, you could jump forever.

Little by little, you no longer needed me.

You became your own person, without me holding your hand, and I resented it.

Yet you didn't forget me. You still loved to talk things over with me, to tell me your secrets, to share your feelings. But we were very different, and I decided that we could not get along.

Do you remember our talks about religion? You insisted that you did not understand, that the Koran verses had nothing to do with you, that centuries had gone by, that the idea of God did not interest you, that you had other things to think about, that all you wanted was to live. Live.

That's all you wanted, Djelila.

I tried to explain that you were wrong. I was arrogant. I was so sure of myself. I was so jealous of you.

Forgive me, Djelila.

But how could you possibly forgive me today?

Stop haunting me, Djelila!

After that slap to your face, the first slap, I ran over to you. I held my hand out for you, but I also rejoiced to see you humiliated.

"Thank you for being there, Sohane. Thank you." This is what you said to me.

I didn't want to admit it that day, but watching the whole scene without even trying to intervene was probably worse than hitting you myself. Nearly every night, Djelila, you live in my dreams. I see myself, side by side with Majid and Youssef, watching them hit you again and again. I do not move. Then I bend down and open a can. A can of gasoline.

Nine

"Your daughters are beautiful, very beautiful."

Uncle Ahmed is leaning back in his chair, rubbing his stomach with satisfaction. Mom did not keep her word. It's almost midnight, and Taïeb and Idriss are still watching a DVD. The rest of us are just finishing dinner. As usual, Mom outdid herself: her tagine was delicious. When I saw how much she had prepared, it looked like there was enough to feed an army, but that wasn't counting Uncle Ahmed. Or Dad. Now Djelila is serving tea. Mom put out three dishes filled with the gazelle horns on the table and one on the rug, near the boys. Mesmerized by the TV screen, Taïeb and Idriss hardly say thank you before they start stuffing themselves.

Uncle Ahmed also helps himself to a horn; he sips his

tea, his mouth filled with biscuit, and looks at us, my sister and me.

"Yes, they are really beautiful, your daughters," he says again.

Dad smiles. He appreciates the compliment.

"If we were back home, you could marry them off. You'd have no trouble finding them good husbands."

Uncle Ahmed's tone seems to indicate that he is joking. But we all know that he believes what he says.

"Aren't we already home?" Djelila asks suddenly.

Everyone turns to look at her.

We have an implicit rule: be respectful of guests. Mom and Dad let us dress the way we want, even let us wear makeup. They allow us to have a drink (as long as it's non-alcoholic) with friends after school. They consented to let Djelila join the basketball team. Simply put, they aren't always on our backs. They trust us. In return, we have to bring home good grades. We're supposed to work studiously. But we have to be discreet when we have company, not stand up to our parents, not draw attention to ourselves. We have to be kind and respectful.

Respect. That is what the Koran teaches us. We started praying with our parents as soon as I turned seven. Djelila was only six, but it made no difference. We loved these moments together. Dad and Mom recited the surahs of the Koran while my sister and I repeated after them. One prayer in the morning, the other ones in the evening. Impossible to do otherwise because of work or school. Then, after I turned thirteen, Mom told us we could go to the mosque by ourselves. Djelila and I talked about it in bed until midnight; we were nervous and excited at the same time. It was an important step. Our parents were granting us a freedom and a responsibility.

I'll never forget the first time we went to the home of Imam Mokthar Benrahmoune without our parents. It was a Friday evening. The muezzin had just made the call for prayer. We had been unable to go to the midday prayer because of school. Mokthar smiled at us discreetly. We removed our shoes, adjusted the scarves that covered our heads, and knelt in the women's corner to pray. It wasn't a real mosque, but that didn't matter. The imam had set aside one room of his apartment for prayer, and he was there to guide us toward God.

Djelila and I used to go there every Friday after school.

One Friday, Djelila came home in a hurry. She told me that she couldn't come to the mosque because she had to catch up on a lesson with one of her friends. She was in ninth grade, and for the first time in many years we weren't at the same school. She promised me she would go the following Monday. This happened several more times, until she simply asked me not to wait for her anymore. Mom and Dad didn't notice right away. In fact, it's probably the imam who told Dad. From then on, whenever I prayed at night, Djelila read a magazine or did her homework.

Even though my sister claims that she doesn't recognize herself in Islam, that she feels distant from all its teachings, she can't possibly have forgotten the notion of respect.

Yet I have the feeling that she's about to break this rule.

41

Her ruddy cheeks and the spark in her dark eyes belie the apparent calm of her face.

Uncle Ahmed furrows his brow. To be on the safe side, he has kept an amused flicker in his eyes. It's always good to have an exit. Being a guest calls for the respect of manners: no scandal in your host's house.

"Your uncle means Algeria," Mom says, as if Djelila had not really understood.

My sister does not back off. "I thought you were born in France, Uncle Ahmed," she says.

It is true that Uncle Ahmed was born in France. Like Dad and Mom. Only Aunt Algia comes from "back home," as Uncle Ahmed calls it. And once a year, he goes to El Aricha, the area in Algeria where his ancestors were born. We have cousins there, cousins I do not know. They are the ones who introduced Uncle Ahmed to Aunt Algia, as the custom requires. She is twelve years younger than he is. They were married in the village, according to tradition. He brought back magnificent photographs. When I saw them I wished I had been at the wedding. All the women were beautifully dressed and made up, the men dancing. I could almost hear the *youyous*.

"Yes, that's right, I was born in France," Uncle Ahmed answers. "But I'm not one of those Arabs who repudiates his roots. France is my second country. Algeria will always be first in my heart!"

Uncle Ahmed has grown a little agitated. He gives Djelila a defiant look.

"Well, I don't feel like an Arab," Djelila counters. "I'm French and proud to be. It's great that Jadi and Hana decided to live here. In France, liberty is a right! I think some Arabs forget that this is France and not Algeria!"

Her tone is so unexpected that Taïeb and Idriss have stopped watching the DVD and turned their attention to us.

Uncle Ahmed stiffens in his chair. He no longer looks at Djelila but at Dad. It is the host's duty to maintain respect.

Dad gets up. He glares at Djelila. She looks down but does not say a word.

"Djelila! How dare you speak to your uncle this way?" Dad says. "Apologize, right now!"

"Djelila, dear, what is the matter tonight?" Mom says, getting into the fray. She approaches Djelila and puts her hand on her forehead. "You're sick, darling. You have a fever."

My sister sighs and looks up.

She is pale now.

"Forgive me, Uncle Ahmed. I did not mean to offend you," she says.

Uncle Ahmed raises an eyebrow. He is satisfied: justice has been served.

"Don't forget, my girl," he says. "It is the whole family and your country of origin that you offend when you speak so."

Djelila nods silently. "Can I go to bed now?" she asks Mom softly. "I'm dead tired."

"Of course, dear."

Djelila leaves the dining table as Uncle Ahmed sips his tea again, and Taïeb and Idriss refocus their eyes on the TV screen.

It is the second time today that my sister has needed me and I have abandoned her.

Ten

Taïeb's and Idriss's voices in the kitchen, closet doors opening and shutting, chair legs squeaking on the linoleum. Dad dragging his slippered feet.

I slept in Djelila's bed last night. In her sheets that haven't been changed. In fact, nothing has changed: her posters of singers, the tiny mirror she used to put her makeup on in the morning, her stuffed bunny, her school supplies, even the magazine she was reading at the time is on the bedside table that we shared. Just as if she were going to come home from school tonight, all smiles, dropping herself onto the blue comforter to tell me all about her day—about her teachers and the gossip in the cafeteria. As if she were going to throw her bags beside the chair and sit at her desk, grumbling about a math problem she needs to solve.

But she will not be back.

Djelila, my sister, is dead. Dead.

Is this the first time I've managed to say it? Is it the first time that I've fully realized it?

Yet there is the slab at the door of the tower.

We had the funeral, with Mom's constant weeping and cries of pain, Dad's hardened face, Taïeb and Idriss with Grandmother Leïla, Hana Leïla, their faces wet with tears.

Before the funeral, the TV news, with their huge cameras and fuzzy microphones and nosy journalists, lurked.

And before that, the police.

And the flames.

That is all I saw: the flames.

Did Majid wait for you after school? Did he follow you the way he did the day he slapped your face? How did he convince you to go to the basement with him? Did he force you? Did he say he needed to talk? Why did you go with him? You thought you were so strong; you said you weren't afraid of those dimwits; you called them dumb, impotent jerks. Is that what you told Majid? Did you insult him? In any case, he had already made up his mind; he probably had a few days earlier. Maybe the desire to murder you had been boiling inside of him ever since he slapped you—ever since the first slap.

He had prepared everything: the gasoline and the matches. You probably had no time to react as he splashed you with the liquid, then struck a match and threw it on you. Right away, you shot into flames and started to scream.

46

If I had come down earlier, would I have been able to save you? Was it still possible? Why did I come down?

To this day, I am unable to answer these questions.

I had just taken a break from my homework. An economics essay, I remember. I was having a hard time. Four books were spread out in front of me and I couldn't understand any of them. It was a nice day. The sun was shining on the square, almost giving it a cheerful appearance. I don't remember deciding to go out, and yet I put my head scarf and jacket on. When I passed the kitchen, I told Mom I was heading out and opened the door. Immediately, I heard your howls. I rushed down the stairs, knowing somehow that it was already too late. I rushed to the basement and saw the flames.

I saw your burnt body fall to the ground.

He was there—the madman. With his can of gasoline and his matches. It was an incredible sight. My eyes saw what had happened, but my mind did not believe it. It wasn't him; it wasn't you. You were not dead, and you had not been burnt alive in the basement of our tower. I could not go to you. You no longer existed. You were just a cremated outline. There was nothing left of what Djelila had been. No hair. No smile. No gazelle eyes. I charged at him then, hitting him with all my strength, my clenched fists landing on his face to make him disappear. Nothing of what I'd seen had happened. You, my sister, were alive. I could love you, hate you, lecture you, console you . . . Djelila!

I'm told I was screaming. I do not remember. I'm told

your murderer was on the ground and that I was pummeling him and shouting incoherently. My cries of pain alerted the tenants of the building that something was horribly wrong, not your cries, Djelila, not yours.

Afterward, everything is a blur.

Silence returns to the apartment. Taïeb and Idriss have left for school. Dad is at work, Mom at the supermarket. One question torments me and causes me intense anguish: how can life go on?

Eleven

I stayed at the table with Uncle Ahmed and Aunt Algia. Mom made another pot of tea and Uncle Ahmed told us stories about his colleagues at work. He has a job at a car dealership where he earns a good living that pays for his yearly trips to Algeria. Aunt Algia doesn't work. She's expecting a baby. Uncle Ahmed's face beams with pride. He's always putting a proprietary hand on his wife's round belly.

I wasn't listening to their conversation. I was simply present, as if to compensate for my sister's attitude and to prove that my father had not failed entirely, that at least one of his daughters wasn't corrupted by the West.

What a joke!

I don't believe a word of it. I've never agreed with Uncle Ahmed. For as long as I can remember, his arrogance has irritated me. Because he's the eldest, he has a way of be-littling my father, of giving him unwanted advice, of underlining his mistakes, of meddling with our education. I would like to snub him as Djelila did. But it's out of the question. I want to appear at my best. For once, Djelila isn't the center of admiration; for once, Dad reprimanded her. I want to take advantage of the situation.

As usual, the last topic of conversation centers on Hana Leïla, my father and uncle's mother.

Uncle Ahmed leans forward and joins his two hands. "Have you been to see Mother these last few days?" he mumbles.

"I went last week, but Saïda paid her a visit yesterday," Dad answers, looking at my mother.

"How was she?" Uncle Ahmed asks, his eyes on Dad, clearly not interested in my mother's opinion.

"In good shape."

My grandmother is far better than in good shape. Hana Leïla will bury us all. But it's not her health that Uncle Ahmed has on his mind. He finds her eccentric. How many times have I heard him advise Dad to watch over her? This amuses Hana Leïla. "My poor son is so sure a woman's sole role is to prepare couscous and to nod when spoken to," she says. "I don't know who he got that from. Not me, that's for sure! It's obvious that he never had to take care of a large family on his own."

Hana Leïla is funny. Djelila and I used to visit her often, before.

Before. Before what? I do not know. Why don't we go over anymore? How come we haven't been since the beginning of the school year? I have to speak to Djelila about it. We have to schedule a visit. It's not difficult: Hana Leïla lives two towers from ours.

"You should watch the company she keeps," Uncle Ahmed warns as he puts his jacket on.

I don't pay much attention. He may be talking about my sister as much as about Hana.

My father nods and Uncle Ahmed goes home with Aunt Algia, who, as always, did not say a word. "She's shy," Mom says. I believe it. Aunt Algia is probably a lot more at ease chatting in the company of women exclusively. And preferably in a kitchen.

The little ones have fallen asleep on the rug. Dad turns the TV off and carries them to bed. I start helping Mom clear the table but she shakes her head.

"Go to bed, dear," she says, smiling. "You're tired too."

She has such a kind smile. I bend toward her—she is so small—and kiss her cheek.

I have only one wish: sleep.

When I enter our bedroom, Djelila isn't undressed. She's sitting cross-legged on her bed, earphones on, shaking her head slowly and mumbling the lyrics of the song she's listening to. Probably some band in one of the posters above her desk. No comment.

I take off my sweater. Then I sit down and remove my shoes.

51

"You know what?" Djelila says. "I'm really fed up."

She takes off her earphones. Her gaze is somber. Nothing velvety tonight in her gazelle eyes.

"Where did you get that iPod?" I ask her.

"A friend lent it to me."

"A friend?"

There is skepticism in my voice. What is happening to me? Do I suddenly think I'm the Taliban police of vice and virtue? I don't. But for a reason I can't explain—don't want to explain—Djelila is getting on my nerves.

I can feel the familiar jealousy bubble to the surface, but I refuse to acknowledge it. Tonight Djelila is responsible for all my anxieties, all my disappointments, all the questions I ask myself, without coming up with answers.

"Axel. Axel lent it to me."

She doesn't protest or tell me to mind my own business. She always answers my questions, a habit from childhood. We were inseparable then. Before. Even if I do not know before what.

"I think they're all a bunch of morons," Djelila says.

"Who are you talking about?"

"I don't know, everybody. Majid and the others, Uncle Ahmed and even Aunt Algia."

I don't say anything. I just frown as I put on the large T-shirt I wear as a nightgown.

"They slapped my face, Sohane. Didn't you see them slap my face?"

Yes, I saw them.

"Majid is the one who slapped you," I point out.

52

"Just the same."

You're probably right, Djelila, it is the same.

"So what has Uncle Ahmed got to do with it?" I ask.

"Didn't you hear him tonight? 'They're beautiful, your daughters. You could already get them married.'"

"So what?" I say with a shrug. "You know how he is. You know how he talks. Just listen. Why pay attention? Besides, I'd like to remind you that Jadi and Hana didn't actually choose to come to France as you claim. External events had something to do with it."

"I don't understand how you can listen to Uncle's macho comments without reacting to them," Djelila says without paying attention to what I've said. "I thought you were a feminist."

Fair enough. I use her ignorance to argue against her, and she reminds me of our discussions. It's true that one of our favorite subjects was feminism. I'm the one who used that big word first.

"Not this way, Djelila. Feminism is not a fight; it's a way of life."

When I'm unsure of myself I wrap my arguments in beautiful sentences. Usually it works, but right now I can't afford to give my sister time to react.

"And do you think your attitude and the way you dress help the feminist cause?" I continue.

"Why do you say that? I thought feminists fought for women's freedom. That's what I demand—my freedom—when I dress the way I do."

I can't help sniggering.

"Is looking like those ads that make men drool—ads that follow all the clichés men impose on us—your way to claim freedom?"

Djelila remains silent. Not because I've convinced her of anything, but because she's surprised by my answer and its vehemence. I've never said anything like this to her.

Actually, I've never said this out loud before. Last time, in French class, when Ms. Lombard made us read the article about Afghanistan, the discussion immediately switched to the right to wear the Islamic veil in France. That was the teacher's intent. She hadn't chosen the article by chance. The law had already been voted on, but that didn't stop the questions. Should it or should it not have been tolerated, that was the discussion. What did it mean? Who was forcing young Islamic girls to cover their hair? The girls argued that they weren't being forced. So then why would a woman agree to it? Because, of course, the veil can only be a way to undermine the freedom of women, a sign of humiliation.

We had a discussion, not a debate, since everybody agreed. They only repeated what we hear on the radio and TV. That's why I kept quiet. Listening to everyone, I quickly understood that I would not be able to declare, as had the others, that I was shocked by the Taliban's actions in Afghanistan. Not while also affirming that forbidding the veil—or the head scarf—seemed to me an infringement on liberty. Besides, with the teacher and the class in consensus, how was I supposed to make myself heard? My arguments were too scattered, too personal.

I've turned these ideas over and over in my mind for a good while, though. Who am I, exactly? Are my goals contradictory? Is it possible to be a woman and Muslim at the same time? What image of myself do I project to those around me? I'm getting tired of my partitioned life: school, the projects, home. I don't feel like myself anywhere anymore. I have friends at school, but we talk about everything and nothing. We aren't really close. I never confide in them, and they don't ask me to. I never see them outside of school. I'm known as a hardworking girl, which I am. A nice girl, no doubt, but I've declined so many invitations to parties that people have stopped asking. I've never spoken to Charlene or Sofia about what is important to me. Nobody knows, for instance, that I am Muslim. Nobody asks. When I refuse a cigarette, nobody cares why. I could explain that my religion prohibits smoking, but who would be interested? It is important. But who can I talk to? My own sister doesn't want to understand me anymore.

I wish the whole world could know what I am. Who I am.

Most journalists talk about what they do not know, about matters they don't take the trouble to understand. They adopt the clichés that suit them—take one aspect of an issue until it becomes a caricature. For them, being a Muslim man means wanting to enslave women, to deny them any rights, any life. I can't say that this isn't a reality. But it's only one reality among many—the one that is best known since it's the one that gets the most media coverage.

All *I* need is to be in sync with my beliefs and religion, even if that seems ridiculous to other girls my age. It's true that I've never gone out with a boy. So what? I have lots of other things to think about for now. Besides, love seems too important to last only three days or even two months. Or does being a teenager mean you have to be frivolous? Should your main interest be the color of your eye shadow, or the clothes you wear? Should whether my thong shows above my jeans be my sole concern? What a fascinating debate, right? Am I strange because all this leaves me indifferent? Actually, I am not indifferent! I am raging mad. I'd like to be able to confide all of my feelings to my sister. To my Djelila. I wish she could understand me. Approve of me. Be like me.

"I've decided to wear a head scarf, Djelila," I tell her.

Djelila's mouth goes slack. Her eyes search mine, trying to decipher whether I'm provoking her, joking, or serious.

"I'm going to wear a head scarf," I repeat.

"What?"

It's almost as if I just announced I'm on drugs!

"I don't understand," Djelila goes on stubbornly.

"I need to feel like myself," I explain. "I need to be respected. I want my beliefs and my choices to be respected. I'm an Arab, Djelila. Arab and Muslim. That is our parents' and our grandparents' religion. . . ."

"True," Djelila says. "But Hana Leïla is Muslim and she doesn't wear a veil. Neither does Mom."

Djelila speaks softly. I hear disbelief in her voice. She is giving up, as if she's suddenly realized to what extent we have become different.

I take her hand. I don't want her to forget we are sisters.

"We already talked about this, Djelila. You know how I hate seeing girls exposing themselves on billboards and in magazines. I don't want to be like them. That's not what it means to be a woman. I need to be respected."

"I want to be respected too," Djelila says. "Without having to disappear or hide my face."

Djelila retrieves her hand. The tension between us is palpable. We are enemies. Enemy sisters.

But it's not what I want.

I would love to make her see things my way. If she were to follow my example, I'm certain she would be happier. And less in danger.

I guess I want to protect you, little sister. But from what?

have become different.

And less in danger.

Twelve

I wanted to protect you, Djelila. But from what?

I have no photograph of you except the ID picture on your public transportation card. It also happens to be the one that appeared in the newspapers. I guess the journalists got it from your registration card at school.

No journalist dared come to our home. Uncle Ahmed was on guard in the lobby of our tower and threatened them, along with anyone whose face he didn't like, anyone who ventured beyond the mailboxes, with a lawsuit. He stayed there three days. Maybe he slept there too. I'm sure he would still be at his post if the police hadn't told him to leave. I watched him walk away, shaking with sobs, his back stooped. Uncle Ahmed was crying in public, without shame. The neighbors shielded him from the prying eyes of the newsmongers.

Eventually I had to go out to buy groceries. I crossed the square to reach the supermarket. Most of the journalists had left after two days. And no one knew my face. Only once did a woman approach me, as if by accident.

She was slim and pretty, with blond hair. "Excuse me . . . ," she said.

"Yes."

My voice was almost hostile. My throat was dry. I hadn't uttered a word for days. I had only hugged Mom and fed Taïeb and Idriss.

"I don't mean to disturb you," the woman said, "but do you live in this tower?"

I almost chose not to answer. The woman—probably twenty-three, twenty-five at most, a news intern maybe—turned red. I cashed in on my advantage and shot her my darkest look.

"I . . . My question may seem indiscreet, but I . . . It's . . . You're very young, aren't you?"

I nodded in spite of myself.

"It's about your veil. I'd like to understand why a young woman chooses to cover her hair as you do."

I am almost certain that her question was personal. Naive and personal.

I smiled. Or rather, I managed a grimace that could be mistaken for a half smile.

"It's not a veil, it's a head scarf."

And as I turned on my heels, paying no more attention to her, I was filled with a strange feeling of satisfaction.

When I returned from the supermarket, a bag in each hand, the woman was interviewing some kids who were playing outside. From the mischievous looks on their faces, they were having fun telling her horrible stories about the projects. They've been doing that ever since the journalists began taking an interest in them. I guess the newsmongers have nothing better to jot down on their pads. The woman glanced at me out of the corner of her eye and quickly bent over her notebook as if to reread some of her very important scribbles.

I smiled inwardly.

Do you remember, Djelila? "It's not a veil, it's a head scarf." Do you remember?

Your ID photo is pinned on the wall above my desk. Your gaze is on me all the time.

In our family, we don't click away with a camera at children from birth through adolescence, from first steps to each birthday, or the vacation on the beach, and all the rest.

Anyway, we never vacationed at the beach, and Dad never owned a camera. Uncle Ahmed has one, but he uses it only in Algeria.

So I don't have any other photos of you, but I do not need one.

When you were four years old, Mom put your hair in pigtails. The barrettes you liked best were sequined plastic butterflies. When we went shopping, we each held one of Mom's hands, and whenever she stopped to look at a dress we didn't like, we would run off and dart between the racks,

and play hide-and-seek in the fitting rooms. Do you remember the day you lifted a curtain and a woman screamed
because she was wearing only her bra? Or was I the one
who lifted the curtain? We ran off quick as lightning. Mom
caught up with us. She hadn't seen anything, but she had
no trouble guessing what had happened. The other shop-
pers and the saleswoman threw her a nasty look that clearly
said "Watch your kids!" Mom dragged us outside, her head
down. She didn't scold us. She was too ashamed of herself
to do that. I don't remember our mother ever raising her
voice. She was too self-conscious, with some sort of inferior-
ity complex she had managed to convince herself was real.
But we weren't sorry for her: we were only six and seven
years old and didn't have a worry in the world. Not like our
mom—we dreamt of a life that we would build, a life in
which no one would step on our feet, in which we would
walk with heads raised. The world had better watch out!

We had our whole lives in front of us.

Djelila.

I wanted to protect you, but from what?

I did not recognize the enemy.

I wanted to protect you, but I let vicious people attack
you. I let Majid and his gang hurt you. I was too sure of
myself. I wanted to protect you; I did not understand.

I was so sure I was right. And if I was right, you had to
be wrong.

Enemy sisters.

I didn't want it to be that way. But the only way to

be close to you again was to put you on the right path. I thought you were lying to yourself, that you were betraying your family, your roots, your God, out of boldness. I was your big sister. And I was going to bring you gently back to reason.

God, forgive me.

Arrogance is a sin.

I wanted to protect you and you are dead.

Djelila.

Thirteen

Djelila is the one to make peace. She can't stand being on bad terms with me. She comes and sits beside me on my bed and puts her head on my shoulder. Her hair is silky, except for the blond strand, which is a little rougher. I stroke it.

"If wearing a head scarf is important to you, Sohane," she murmurs, "you should do it." After a while, she adds, "But you know, you're going to run into trouble. Head coverings are forbidden at school."

I gesture dismissively.

"You can't forbid people to be who they are and to think what they think," I say. "I don't want to convert anyone. I just want to be me."

Djelila snuggles closer. When we were little, we

sometimes slept in the same bed. I always loved her smell and the warmth of her skin.

"Do you remember, Djelila, when you wanted to be a princess?"

She laughs noiselessly. "Nothing has changed; I still want to be a princess. You'll see, one day a prince will come and take me away. He'll have a white horse and—"

"Garments of light," I finish for her.

"Yes, exactly."

Garments of light. Djelila always loved this expression. We discovered it in one of the stories I read to her. She always wanted me to read her stories, so I used to go to the small library in the neighborhood and choose picture books with beautiful illustrations.

"And he'll whisk me off on his horse and I'll have a beautiful white dress as light as snowflakes."

"Djelila . . ."

My sister smiles. "What? You think I'm too old?"

I shrug.

"And you," Djelila declares, "you wanted to be a scientist. After you read the biography of Marie Curie, you wanted to find a vaccine that would save the world!"

It takes her no more than thirty seconds to get undressed: she keeps on her T-shirt, her underwear, and, as usual, her socks. She hates having cold feet. She lies down and tucks herself in under my comforter. I quickly remove my bra, put on the T-shirt that I wear at night, get rid of my jeans, and lie down next to her.

This is how I find you again, little sister.

It's just as if you were never lost.

"It's been a long time since we went to visit Hana Leïla," Djelila whispers.

I close my eyes. "True."

"We could go there after school tomorrow. What time are you done?"

"At four."

"Cool. I finish at three. I could wait for you at the Green Handkerchief."

The Green Handkerchief is the closest café to school. It's a convenient meeting place for Racine students.

"OK."

I hesitate before asking, "You don't have anything to do after school tomorrow?"

Djelila shakes her head. "No, nothing. We'll meet at the Hanky and go together to Hana's, OK?"

"Sure."

I can't help thinking that Djelila has found herself a bodyguard. There is no way Majid and the others will dare approach her if we are together.

Djelila has fallen asleep beside me. Her breath is steady. She even snores lightly.

When I wake up in the morning, she is already out of bed. Her hair is tousled, but she's dressed. She shoves her books and notebooks into her schoolbag.

She yawns as I rub my eyes.

"Don't bother asking me if I fell off the bed," she grumbles. "Because I did, you space hog."

My alarm clock indicates 6:54. Usually Djelila stays

in bed as long as possible. I pick my pillow up from the ground. It probably fell when Djelila toppled onto the floor.

"You haven't changed your mind, have you?" she asks.

I frown. "Changed my mind about what?"

"About the veil . . . ."

"Not the veil, Djelila, the head scarf."

"What's the difference?"

"The difference is in the word. I don't want to wear a veil to hide myself from others' eyes. . . ."

"From men, you mean."

"Well, if you want to put it that way. It doesn't matter. I'm not ashamed to be a woman. All I want is to show my beliefs. I want them to be recognized. They're a part of me."

"OK, OK. So what are you going to cover your head with then?"

I hadn't thought about it.

"Not with one of Mom's old things, I hope."

"I don't know, I—"

"Here, use this!"

Djelila throws a silky and colorful scarf on the bed, one she bought at the flea market last summer.

I feel like bursting out laughing.

"I can't wear that," I tell her.

My sister's shoulders collapse. "I know."

"I think I have what I need."

I get dressed and open a dresser drawer. I have the two top drawers, my sister the bottom two. I take out a square off-white cotton scarf.

"Hmm. At least it's not black," Djelila mumbles.

I go over to the tiny mirror hanging between the two posters on Djelila's wall. I fold the square in half before I put it on my hair. It's not very large. I'll have to find something better. I decide to go to the supermarket after school. Meanwhile, I tie the scarf under my chin, trying to cover my neck as much as possible. Obviously, it will not stay in place like this for long.

"Djelila, can you hand me the hairpins on my desk?" I ask.

"You know, it's not that ugly," she answers.

I turn and face my sister. She has put the colorful scarf that she offered to lend me on her head. It's tied up nicely, and she's making faces as she tries to see herself in the mirror.

"One good thing is that if you wake up with a pimple on your forehead or neck, it won't show with this."

"Djelila . . ."

She shrugs, removes her scarf, and hands me the hairpins.

"Of course, better not to have a pimple on the tip of your nose . . . unless you live in Afghanistan."

I attach my scarf with three hairpins. I'm almost pleased with the result. Strangely enough, I have the feeling Djelila is afraid. Of what? I wonder. Why should she be more afraid for me than I am for her when she wears a T-shirt that exposes her navel?

"Don't you feel weird?" she asks.

Absolutely not. I feel relieved. The image the mirror reflects is, at last, the one I have of myself.

"Hurry up, Dje, we're going to be late," I say.

It has been forever since I've called my sister "Dje."

It is past seven-thirty. We had better hurry. I won't bother with breakfast this morning either.

"Wait."

Djelila is putting on makeup—always the same lines of kohl, one under each eye, another fine one on her eyelids, mascara, and a bit of gloss on her lips. Then she brushes her hair vigorously.

"I have to untangle my hair since I'm not hiding it," she tells me.

No comment. I grab my book bag and open the door of our room. I hear Dad's electric razor from the bathroom. Mom is giving Taïeb and Idriss their breakfast in the kitchen.

I walk in.

"You're pretty, Sohane," Idriss says.

Taïeb shakes his head. "I don't like it."

As soon as Idriss voices an opinion, Taïeb says the opposite. Mom looks at me with a strange spark in her eyes. Is she surprised? I don't think so. Is she proud? Maybe a little. It's hard to tell. I've never seen Mom wear a head scarf. Suddenly I wonder why, but I don't dare ask.

"You look very nice, Sohane," she says.

"Thanks, Mom. We have to go or we'll be late."

"Morning, Mom," Djelila says, walking in behind me. Quickly, she kisses Mom's cheek, then grabs a piece of buttered toast from the table.

"Hey, that's not yours!" Idriss shouts.

"It's mine now," Djelila answers.

"You're lovely too," Mom says as she pats my sister's cheek. "Go now. Be good."

We take the stairs four at a time and run across the lawn of the square. The bus is there and we jump on.

Djelila sits next to me. We put our bags on the floor and prop our knees against the glass partition.

The landscape goes by. Towers, parking lots, kids riding their bikes on sidewalks.

Karine and Estelle board the bus. Djelila waves to them but doesn't get up. She stays seated beside me. She even turns to me.

"What's your first class?" she asks.

"French."

"Ah. OK."

"You?"

What a strange way to talk to each other! It feels awkward, self-conscious, artificial. Have we gotten totally out of the habit of speaking to each other in public?

"Umm . . . History with that stupid guy."

"You mean Ducasse. I always thought he was funny."

School.

We get off the bus side by side. Djelila leans toward me and gives me a kiss on the cheek.

"Don't forget we're meeting up at the Hanky this afternoon."

"No, I won't. See you at four o'clock."

"Yeah, at four."

Djelila walks off. This morning I get the feeling she wants to make a declaration to the whole world: "This is my sister! This girl with a scarf on her head is my sister!"

Fourteen

"It's my sister."

Djelila, my sister.

Your name is engraved on a slab that is surrounded by grass. A commemorative slab the town hall paid for.

You wanted to be a princess, Djelila. You had magnificent dreams. Of course, I would make fun of you.

We used to invent games by the hundreds. Our imaginations had no limit. Our bedroom was a castle, a ship, a forest swarming with monsters, a jungle. . . . . .

Once, when you were seven and I was eight, two tigers attacked us. We had to kill them to save our lives. Then we discovered that they had a cub. We took it with us, you bottle-fed him, and he became loyal to us. Do you remember, Djelila? He became our protector.

Why did you grow up, Djelila? You were pretty with your butterfly barrettes.

Our games often ended in arguments. When I wanted to conquer a new country, you would meet a charming prince and demand to get married.

"Djelila, it's not fun if you get married," I would say.

"Please, Sohane. I'll get married, then I'll come back with you into the jungle."

"No. I know all you'll do is take care of your Prince Charming!"

"Sohane, I promise you I won't. Come to my wedding. Then you and I will leave together."

"Adventurers don't need to get married!"

"Then I won't play anymore!"

"I don't care. I don't need you!"

"Too bad. You always want to be in charge!"

So I would lie down on my bed and read a book, ignoring you, and you would sulk. You would go to the kitchen and help Mom cook the meal, complaining about me the whole time. "Sohane doesn't want to play with me anymore," you would whine. "She always lets me down." And as Mom peeled vegetables or stirred a sauce, she would tell you stories about when she was young, with her sister. She always managed to make you laugh.

My sister would come back, lie down next to me, and put her head on my shoulder. She couldn't stand having us mad at each other.

I never rejected her.

Time goes by. Without you.

I try not to think. I try to focus solely on my lessons. I have only one desire: to leave this place. I went into Paris last week, to pick up the famous *Student Connection Guide* at the main university center in the city. The guy at the reception desk told me at least four times that my school was going to distribute the guide shortly and not to worry. I finally got frustrated and told him that I wasn't attending school anymore, that I was studying by correspondence. He looked at my head scarf knowingly and muttered, "I understand," then kindly started to explain each paragraph of the application form. I listened patiently, without really hearing him. I had already obtained all the necessary information by phone, and I had all the documents required to fill out the scholarship and residence application forms.

I'm beginning to have a knack for filling out applications. Since enrolling in correspondence courses, I've had to sort through all sorts of forms: registration forms to courses by mail, where you have to make sure to answer all questions if you want to receive the lessons in a timely fashion; forms to take the French and biology exams, where you can't overlook anything if you want to be admitted to the test room; forms for the graduation certificate . . .

I asked him where I could find computers with Internet access and he showed me, saying, "You're lucky. One of them is just freeing up." I thanked him.

I had to fill in all the blanks. Name, surname, address. I had already calculated my tuition based on my parents'

75

income taxes. I would receive about 250 euros a month and I would be entitled to a room on campus. I would be fine. A new life was opening up in front of me. As soon as school starts again, I will be in Paris. I will no longer be Sohane Chebli, sister of Djelila Chebli, the girl who was burnt alive in the basement of the Lilac housing project.

I also had to indicate how many dependents my parents were providing for. I wrote four.

I try to forget you, to escape you, but everything brings me back to you, Djelila.

I can't take it any longer. I can't look at your posters or at your bed anymore. I can't look at your blue comforter, at the pair of socks rolled into a ball at the foot of your bed.

You always wore socks to bed. You hated to have cold feet.

Nothing has been moved. Nothing.

I wanted it that way.

The doorbell rings. I am alone in the apartment. Mom and Dad are at work. The boys are in school.

Is it Mrs. Achouri again with a cake? She says she comes to offer "comfort," but I know her eyes take in the state of our despair so she can feed the gossipmongers in front of the mailboxes.

I get up, determined to be less polite than last time, and open the door. There are five of them. I recognize them all. Djelila talked about them all the time, and I watched them often in the schoolyard. Also, they have come before.

Sylvan, Karine, Estelle, Jerome, and Basil. A delegation. They never came to see Djelila, not even to pick her up to go out. The dividing lines had been drawn. Neither my sister nor I had ever invited friends over.

Karine is the one who starts talking.

"Hi, Sohane."

"Hello."

My answer is anything but welcoming.

"We'd like to talk to you."

The first time they came, Mom opened the door. It was just a few days after Djelila died. Her death made the front pages of newspapers. They printed theories, created facts, spitting their lies and using all the gossip they could pick up here and there: *Djelila, Age 16, Murdered by her Boyfriend. Djelila Chebli: Violence in the Projects. Tragedy in the Lilac Housing Project: Racism Is Alive. The Djelila Affair: Crime of Passion or Politics? Dead Because of a Slap.* And of course, the unavoidable, *The Rise of Islam in the Projects.*

Karine had spoken for all of them at that time too. Her eyes were red and swollen. They all had red and swollen eyes. Mom had not invited them in. She simply hadn't thought to. I had stayed in the corridor.

"We came to offer our condolences, Mrs. Chebli. For Djelila."

Mom had looked at them lifelessly, as if she didn't understand what they were talking about. She turned her head, her face distraught, glancing at me, then at Dad, who was crumpled in his living room armchair. Prostrate with grief.

"Thank you," Mom had mumbled as she started to push the door closed.

"Mrs. Chebli—"

Mom didn't listen to the rest, probably hadn't even heard what they said. She had shut the door.

"What? What do you want to talk about?" I ask Karine today.

My voice is hostile, almost in spite of myself. Why do I resent them? Is it because they are alive, go to school, laugh, love?

Estelle and Sylvan are holding hands.

Karine takes a deep breath. "It's almost nine months since Djelila died," she says.

She pauses. I do not speak.

"We'd like to commemorate the anniversary of her death."

"Of her murder," I say.

"Yes, of her murder."

"Why?"

"So that no one forgets it."

Estelle speaks now. "We want everyone to remember Djelila, her joy and laughter," she says. "We loved her, you know, Sohane. We loved her."

It's probably true. Estelle is about to cry, but she goes on.

"We also want to make sure that no one forgets her awful death—her murder, as you just said. We don't want anyone to forget the atrocity of the crime."

78

I shake my head. "I don't want my sister's death to be used as the rallying point for your cause!" I yell.

"That's not what we want. All we want is to express our love. . . ."

Estelle is crying now.

"I'm busy."

"Sohane . . ."

"I'm busy."

That is all I manage to say. I want them to go away. They have no right to grieve. I do not grant them permission to shed tears over my sister, my treasure, my gazelle.

I close the door gently. I do not slam it. I lean my back against it and let myself slide down slowly. I am seated on the floor, in the entryway. But I am not crying.

Fifteen

I approach the gate. They all turn toward me—Lola, Sofia, Christian, and Charlene—and stare in surprise.

"Hi, Sohane."

No one is going to ask me the question.

The bell rings. Charlene and Christian put out their cigarettes against the wall.

"Get to class!"

I can feel furtive glances as I walk across the schoolyard. But everyone's curiosity is short-lived, as if they are embarrassed, or maybe they know that trouble is about to descend on the school. Each of them must be thinking, *I've heard about this on the news; now it's here at Racine High. We're going to see some action!*

I have to admit that it's more difficult than I thought. I

feel ill at ease with so many eyes on me, and the head scarf keeps me warm, too warm. My skull is itchy, and the scarf's edges tickle my neck. In the hall, I hear whispers as I walk by, but they die down.

I enter my classroom and take my usual seat near the window, not too close to the blackboard, not too far either.

Sofia sits near me. If I have one friend at school, it's her. She seems to hesitate a second, then leans toward me.

"You're wearing the veil?" she asks.

"A head scarf," I correct her.

"What?"

"I'm wearing a head scarf."

Sofia gives me an inquiring look. I already feel too tired to explain.

"Why?" Sofia asks softly.

"I'm Muslim."

Sofia keeps silent a moment.

"I know you're Muslim," she says, "but you can't wear that. A law was passed."

Ms. Lombard just walked in, impeccably groomed as always. Today she's wearing an elegant sweater over a pencil skirt. She smiles. I like her even though she's a tough grader. She closes the door behind her. Gradually, the whispers stop. She puts her briefcase on her desk, lifts her head, smiles again—until her eyes land on me.

"Ms. Chebli."

"Yes, ma'am."

"Please take off your head covering."

Everyone turns to look at me. The silence is dense. My face is on fire. I do not budge.

"Ms. Chebli, I asked you to remove your veil."

"You mean my scarf," I say.

How could I have been so naive as to imagine for one second that my decision would be without consequences? I guess I didn't want to think about it. I thought my good faith would speak for me. Also, they know me at school: they know I'm not here to proselytize. I believed that after a few whispers, my head scarf would go unnoticed.

Was I fooling myself?

"I don't understand, Ms. Chebli. What are you trying to prove?"

"Nothing, ma'am."

My cheeks are still red-hot, but I look straight into the teacher's eyes.

"We've already discussed this very topic in class. Have you forgotten the Afghan women who are prisoners in their burkas? Don't you feel a responsibility toward them and all the women of the world?"

Ms. Lombard has raised her voice. She's getting carried away. She's not really expecting an answer from me. All she wants is a sign, a gesture of agreement. But what kind of answer can I possibly give to such a closed-minded and intellectually dishonest question?

"I really don't understand you, Sohane!" Ms. Lombard goes on. "You're a brilliant student. You've never tried to make yourself conspicuous. You're a hardworking girl. You can't jeopardize your future because of such a stupid decision!"

I do not flinch. I do not respond.

"Ms. Chebli, I'm asking you for the last time to remove your veil. In the name of freedom, I cannot tolerate this in my class!"

If I weren't so nauseated, I would snigger at this last declaration.

Never mind. I haven't taken my books out of my bag yet. All I have to do is put my jacket back on and leave.

The teacher bites her lip.

"Sofia, please accompany your friend to Mrs. Desbeaux."

I am almost at the door when Sofia catches up with me. I open the door and go out. Sofia shuts the door behind us.

Our footsteps echo loudly in the deserted corridor. We hear the voices of teachers, a cough, a laugh. The chief educational advisor's office is in the other building.

"You should think about what you're doing, Sohane," Sofia says.

Sofia has accelerated her steps to keep pace with mine. She puts her hand on my arm.

"Sohane . . ."

I stop and look at her.

"Yes, Sofia, I'm listening."

"So?"

"So, I've already thought about it. I'm Muslim."

As I say these words, I realize how sudden and stubborn my decision has been. But I do not want to justify myself.

Sofia does not reply. Her hand is still on my arm. I wish I could thank her.

Mrs. Desbeaux's office is only a few feet away.

"You don't have to come with me, Sofia. Don't worry, I'm not going to flee or go home without permission."

"I trust you."

"Good."

Sofia turns around while I hold my breath. It will surely be easier for me to face the advisor without a chaperone.

I knock on the door.

"Come in."

I enter. Mrs. Desbeaux is sitting behind her desk, filling out papers. She does not look up right away. I wait.

"Ms. Chebli?" she finally says. "What brings you here?"

"I've been expelled from French class, ma'am."

Mrs. Desbeaux immediately sizes up the situation.

"Don't tell me you're surprised, Sohane," she chides me. "You are aware of the law, aren't you?"

Her tone is patronizing and humiliating. It's barely eight-twenty, less than an hour since I got to school, and no one has really taken an interest in *me*. I'm merely a head scarf. Where is Sohane Chebli? She has disappeared; she no longer exists. Instead, everyone sees only a teenager seeking attention and scandal. Overnight I have become the symbol of a population born of immigrants. I'm suddenly adrift— the victim of the rise of fundamentalism. It's possible that some girls started to wear head scarves just to attract attention, or because they were manipulated. But why is it that no one bothers to talk to me without assuming that my choice is stupid or that I just want to antagonize everyone? "I am Sohane Chebli!" I feel like shouting. "Look at *me*! Look at Sohane Chebli."

But it is useless.

"I suppose Ms. Lombard asked you to uncover your head and you refused?" Mrs. Desbeaux asks, seemingly resigned. It's as if she's been expecting to deal with this kind of problem for a while. And she has a strategy at the ready.

"Yes, that's correct."

She takes a pen and scribbles a few words on a piece of paper.

"Go to study hall until nine o'clock. What's your next class?"

"Econ with Mr. Roussin."

She nods. "I'll take advantage of the next thirty minutes to talk to Mr. Roussin. I'll let you know what we decide. For now, a meeting with the principal seems a must. Do you have anything to say to justify your attitude?"

I shrug. My attitude seems obvious, but to explain it in words . . .

"I just want to be me. I don't want to be ashamed of being Muslim and of practicing my religion. I'd like people to accept that. I don't intend to harm anyone."

I blurt all this out without taking a breath and try to keep my eyes fixed on hers.

She sighs.

"I've made note of it, Sohane. You can go."

Study hall is almost empty. The supervisor puts Mrs.

Desbeaux's note on her desk without even reading it and tells me to sit down.

Everything feels unreal—and yet so real at the same time.

I can't believe this is happening. They can't do this to me. They're bluffing—just trying to scare me. But deep down I know that's not true. I'm going to be expelled. They're going to get rid of me as if I have a contagious disease.

Strangely enough, time goes by quickly.

At nine, Mrs. Desbeaux walks in and comes straight to me. She looks somber.

"I spoke to Mr. Roussin," she says. "He insists on abiding by the law and backs Ms. Lombard's decision. He will not admit you in his class as long as you wear the head scarf. Have you given it more thought?"

I hold my breath before answering. "I want to keep my head covered."

Mrs. Desbeaux rolls her eyes. "I didn't think you were so stubborn, Sohane. I can understand your desire to cover your hair—after all, it's your business—but you cannot do so at school. The law is the law. Wouldn't it be enough to wear your head scarf outside?"

"That's not the way it works."

"Do you realize that you're putting your future at risk?"

I can't help thinking, *You're the one putting my future at risk, not me.*

"And Mr. Lhermitte?" I ask. She must have spoken to the principal as well.

"You've got to understand, Sohane. Like us, the principal

is obliged to follow the law. What's more, he fears that your attitude might incite others. He's afraid other girls at school will decide to follow your example. He can't risk having to deal with this problem on a large scale."

A contagious disease. I was right.

I'm scared now. Terrified. They are going expel me for sure. I still have time to back down, to accept Mrs. Desbeaux's suggestion that I remove my head scarf. I open my mouth. Suddenly I regret ever having decided to cover my head. I have a grudge against Djelila without knowing exactly why. All it would take is one word to rewind everything. I can continue to divide myself, playing different parts: Sohane, daughter of Mr. and Mrs. Chebli; Sohane from the Lilac housing projects; Sohane, senior at Racine High School; Sohane the Muslim; Sohane who wears a head scarf and who removes it. . . . But why?

"It's a matter of respecting others, Sohane," Mrs. Desbeaux says.

And what about respecting me?

No. It's too late to renounce my beliefs and desires. I cannot deny my true self.

"What happens now?"

"You'll stay in study hall until the end of the day. We'll call your parents this evening and ask them to come in."

"Can I go to the library instead?" I ask.

"You may."

She agrees willingly. She knows that if I stay in study hall I'll come into contact with lots of students. In the library, there's less chance of my contaminating anyone.

* * *

I decide to sit in a remote corner of the library. Ms. Fleury has obviously been made aware of the situation. She doesn't make any comment. She doesn't even say hello.

I take out my economics book as well as my notepad. I've got an essay due next week. It doesn't matter that I'll no longer be here; I have nothing else to do. It will make the time go by faster.

I give a start when Sofia sits down next to me. I glance at my watch. Twelve o'clock.

"How's it going?" she asks.

I fill her in, telling her what Mrs. Desbeaux said. Sofia doesn't comment.

"Everybody is talking about you, of course."

I shrug. "It'll pass."

"Maybe, but right now you're the most popular person at school!"

I don't even want to know details. I just think that if everybody is talking about me, then Djelila must know what has happened. She hasn't come to see me.

"I have to go," Sofia says. "Do you want something?"

My stomach is crying out for food, but I shake my head.

Sofia leaves. I'm grateful that she didn't try to make me change my mind.

"Hey, *psst!*"

I turn around. It's Djelila. She's hiding behind the shelves and signals me over.

"What are you doing here?" I ask.

"I just heard about you."

"I guessed that. Why are you hiding?"

"I was afraid they wouldn't let me talk to you."

I smile. "I'm not under house arrest yet," I tell her.

Djelila takes two apples, three pieces of cheese, and four or five slices of bread out of her jacket pockets and deposits them on the table. From where she stands, Ms. Fleury can't see us. Fortunately.

"I thought you'd be hungry, so I picked this up in the cafeteria," Djelila says.

"Thanks."

"You're not too afraid?"

"Actually, I am."

Djelila hugs me and puts a hand on my scarf. I almost forgot about it.

"Can you still meet me at four?" she asks.

"Yes, four o'clock at the Hanky. I'll be there."

Djelila winks. "Good. And I'll visit you again later on."

"OK. But don't worry about me."

"Of course I worry about you, Sohane. You're my big sister."

Sixteen

I, too, was worried—worried about you, Djelila.

Your friends haven't left. I can hear them whispering on the landing.

I have not moved.

Maybe because I can't move anymore.

My mind is swimming with memories that weigh heavily in the pit of my stomach and prevent me from moving. My arms, legs, head—my entire body is as heavy as lead. I could stay here. I could stay here forever.

There was a period when you were about eleven or twelve when you were often sick. Never anything serious, but with a high-enough fever to make Mom keep you home. At night, you coughed and I would get up to hold you in my arms. You nestled against me. I would put my hand on your forehead.

"I'll get you a glass of water," I would say.

Before bringing it to your lips, I would press it against your cheeks to cool them.

"Thank you, Sohane," you managed to say before a new coughing fit started.

I was scared for you. When you dozed off, I tried to stay awake to check on your breathing, but I ended up falling asleep too.

In the morning, you were calm. Usually you were asleep when I left for school. I knew that Mom had already used all of her sick days and couldn't stay home anymore. She had to go to work. She wasn't absent long, just between eleven and three o'clock, for her job at the hospital. So I would come back home at lunchtime. I devised a system so I could sneak out of school without being spotted. At twelve sharp, I dashed out of class so I'd be the first to reach the cafeteria, but I didn't eat. On my tray, I put things that would fit easily in my pockets—bread, cheese, fruit—and then I slipped out and ran as quickly as possible away from school. It wasn't too difficult, because at that time of day the supervisors were busy checking on the cafeteria and schoolyard. I ran all the way home. I was out of breath. You were waiting for me. You knew I wouldn't let you down. We ate together on your bed and I told you what had happened at school. You laughed and coughed. I put my hand on your forehead, just like Mom would have done, to make sure your temperature hadn't spiked. I gave you your medicine, and then I ran back to school so I wouldn't miss my first afternoon class. We never told anyone. It was our secret.

Now it is only mine. And it is heavy, so heavy to bear.

After you recovered, Mom took you to the doctor. "She's a bit on the thin side, this little one," the doctor had said with a smile. Back at home, you told me what he said because it upset you. You asked me over and over if I thought you were too skinny. What could I say: you had no butt, no breasts, and your arms and legs were like twigs. On top of that, you had grown about four inches in a few months. All I said was "You're very pretty, Dje, you know that. Everyone says so." This reassured you for about fifteen minutes before you started up again: "It's not fair. Why do you have breasts and I don't?" The doctor recommended athletic activity for you, which is the reason Dad and Mom let you start basketball. Right away you loved it. It was the first time you did something without me.

Your friends' hushed conference is still going on outside the door. What can they be talking about? Do they intend to ring the bell again? Why do they insist on this memorial? My cheeks are almost dry now, just a bit sticky. Slowly I stand up. They don't get it: if there is a memorial, it will mean that you are dead.

Seventeen

Mrs. Desbeaux was determined to have a discussion with me. She came to the library at ten to four, just as I was packing up.

"How was your day, Sohane?" she asked.

I stared at her. Did she expect that a day of isolation had made me change my mind?

"It was fine, thank you."

"Are you planning on wearing your head scarf to school tomorrow?"

"I don't know if I'll come to school at all," I tell her.

Mrs. Desbeaux bites her lower lip. What? Isn't it better for everybody if I don't show up? A relief?

"You can't skip your classes this way, Sohane."

"I might be sick."

I didn't feel like talking to her this morning, and I feel even less like it this afternoon. I can almost hear the clock ticking. Djelila has been waiting for me the past hour at the Green Hanky. I'm in a hurry.

"Well, in any case, we'll call your parents this evening. What time do they get home?"

"My father gets home at seven-thirty, but my mother should already be there. She works part-time."

"Very well."

Mrs. Desbeaux does not move—she looks as if she's expecting me to say something more. I close my bag and put on my jacket.

"Sohane . . ."

"Please excuse me," I say. "I have an appointment at four o'clock and I need to go."

I walk across the library without looking back. I run down the stairs and glance at my watch: just after four. I hope Djelila hasn't left. When I reach the café I'm out of breath. Djelila is there: I can see her, reading, by the window. She waited for me and she's alone. I was afraid that she might be with her school friends and that they would pepper me with questions. I go in and she looks up, smiles at me, and puts her book down. I sit opposite her, still out of breath.

"Do you think they've already called Mom?" she asks me all of a sudden.

I catch my breath. "No, but it won't be long before they do."

"You want to have a coffee, or should we go?"

Djelila is already up. She puts a few bills on the table. All her gestures are so normal. She is at ease. I feel like I'm lagging behind. But I get up too.

We go out and walk side by side, silently. The closer we get to Hana's, the more apprehensive I become. It's like having a boulder growing in the pit of my stomach. The day's events could justify this feeling, but I know there's another reason for it.

"What do you think Hana will say when she sees your head scarf?" Djelila asks.

I shrug, trying to look unconcerned. "Nothing. What can she say?"

Djelila doesn't answer.

We get to our grandmother's tower and open the lobby door, which looks exactly like the one in our building. Hana Leïla's apartment is on the ground floor. Djelila rings the bell. We hear footsteps coming toward the door, as well as music and women's voices. The door opens.

"Djelila! Sohane! *Salaam alaikum!*" Hana greets us. She gathers us in a hug.

Our grandmother must be more than sixty years old, and she is beautiful. She wears her hair short and colors it, which brings out the copper tone of her skin. She has high cheekbones, dark and shiny eyes. She wears a sweater, jeans, and babouches on her feet. Her apartment always looks festive, probably because of the colorful rugs covering the floor, the silver teapot that occupies place of pride on a shelf, and her collection of dolls made of multicolored felt and wool. When we were little girls, Djelila and I loved these dolls. And we loved hearing Hana Leïla tell us about their stories while we played with them. Her mother back in Algeria made the dolls from scraps of fabric. She drew their eyes, which are mostly faded now, with kohl that she almost tattooed onto the fabric. Their earrings were made from a broken, recycled bracelet. When they danced, the earrings jingled merrily. And how they danced—first in Hana Leïla's hands and then in ours.

Our grandmother has company, which adds to the festive atmosphere. The silver teapot sits on the coffee table, along with tea glasses filled with a tawny and mint-perfumed liquid. The huge radio Uncle Ahmed gave her for her last birthday plays exotic music that reminds me of a tale from *The Thousand and One Nights*. When I was little and visited Hana Leïla in her apartment, I imagined I was entering the palace of a sultan, just like the ones in the stories I read to Djelila.

Hana Leïla's friends get up to greet us. They all speak at once and exclaim how lovely and tall we are: "You must be so proud, Leïla." "This little one is your spitting image!" We sit down, smiling from ear to ear. We have the feeling Hana was expecting us.

She pours a glass of tea for each of us. Djelila sits comfortably on the sofa and brings the gold-rimmed glass to her lips. I'm sitting on the edge of a chair and I, too, sip the sugary liquid.

"You've met Malika and Nadja before," Hana Leïla says, "but you don't know Fatiha, my new neighbor. She moved in last November to the apartment right above mine."

Fatiha is probably the same age as Hana Leïla. Her face is more etched, more wrinkled. Her eyes are rimmed with kohl and her wrists are covered with clanging bracelets. She smiles and hums along with the music. At her feet, between her legs, sits a *darbuka*.

"Fatiha is a musician," Hana Leïla explains when she notices me glance at the instrument. "We're in the middle of planning a show."

"A show?" I say.

Djelila looks as surprised as I am.

"Yes, a show to benefit the community center," Malika says proudly.

Malika is the youngest of the four women. She's very likely in Mom's generation, even if it feels as if they were born on different planets. Mom would never dress the way Malika does, in a pair of stretch jeans and sneakers. She would never bleach or tease her hair.

"Fatiha plays the *darbuka*," Hana Leïla explains. "Malika and Nadja dance and sing, and I play the castanets."

She sounds as excited as a four-year-old about to take part in a school show.

"It's going to be a great party," Nadja adds as she shakes her henna-reddened hair. "We've invited everyone in the towers. They'll all bring something to eat and drink."

"No alcohol, of course," Fatiha says as she lights a cigarette.

Hana Leïla waves away the smoke. "Ah, you're polluting the air!" she complains.

Fatiha doesn't answer and takes a puff.

99

"What's the occasion for the party?" asks Djelila.

"See how young people are nowadays!" Nadja cries. "They need a reason to throw a party!"

"The party is the occasion," my grandmother answers with her sunny smile. "But we're talking about ourselves, which is rude. What news do you girls bring? How is school?"

"And the boyfriends?" Fatiha inquires with a wink.

School, boyfriends. Djelila gives me a glance. She's about to speak when Hana Leïla cuts her short.

"Since when do you wear the hijab, Sohane?"

Her expression is serious.

"Since today."

"Today?"

"Yes."

Only the sound of the music fills the apartment now. Djelila sits up.

"Sohane has the right to wear a head scarf if she wants to," my sister says. "It doesn't hurt anyone."

Hana Leïla shakes her head. "No, of course not. I'm just surprised," she says. "You have to be careful—very careful—with religion, as you know, girls."

I nod.

"My granddaughter started wearing the hijab last year," Nadja says. "She's older than you are, Sohane, but I don't understand it. Now she even refuses to shake hands with visitors who come to her home. Her parents have tried to reason with her, but she won't change her mind!"

"I don't get it either," Fatiha joins in. "I lived in Algeria until I was twenty-five and my mother never wore the veil, and *hamdullah*. And she wouldn't want me wearing them either! My mother wanted us to be rid of this custom. She wanted us to be happy, to have fun, not to be hidden behind a veil."

"I don't feel hidden," I manage to mumble.

Hana Leïla puts her hand on mine.

"No, Sohane. You make your own choices, of course. *Inshallah*. Our past has nothing to do with your present, but be careful, my dear, be careful anyway."

I bite my cheek. Djelila looks at her feet.

Fatiha gets up abruptly. "Come on, what's all this about? We're not going to spend the whole afternoon on this topic. These young girls came here expecting hospitality and warmth, and here we are giving them morality lessons. I've had three husbands and twelve children, of which eight are girls, so I feel I know that each one of us has to find her own path, and that it shouldn't keep us from laughing, singing, and dancing together."

"Three husbands and twelve children?" Djelila says in disbelief.

Hana Leïla laughs. "I have the feeling the number increases every day," she says as she gets up to turn up the volume on the radio.

I think again about Uncle Ahmed the other evening and how he worries about his mother. He probably meant the company his mother keeps. I doubt that he likes Fatiha very much.

Malika and Nadja are on their feet now. They begin to dance, swinging their hips like belly dancers. Fatiha has secured her *darbuka* under her left arm and beats on it in rhythm with the music from the radio. Hana Leïla takes the castanets that were on a table and begins to play as she too dances. The sparkling smiles of the women warm the apartment. But my uneasiness has not disappeared. Not at all. It would take more than this, but when Nadja takes my hands to make me get up and dance with her, I don't resist. Fatiha attaches a bell-fringed scarf around my sister's hips. The music fills my body and my heart. We don't move nearly as well as our elders, but I don't care. The pins start to slip off my head scarf, so I remove it and put it on the armrest of the sofa. I am not supposed to wear it here anyway. We are among women.

Nadja, Malika, Fatiha, and Hana Leïla start to sing. I take my sister's hands and dance with her. She laughs. Her hair covers her face. I wish the anxiety in the pit of my stomach would vanish with your laughter, Djelila.

Eighteen

Vanish with your laughter.

Your friends are heading down the stairs. They've given up. I can go lock myself in my bedroom again.

They gave up more easily than the first time, when they got together about the petition.

When we got home that evening after our visit to Hana Leïla's, Mrs. Desbeaux had already called. Dad wasn't back yet. Mom was biting her nails.

"What's all this about, Sohane?" she asked. "They're talking about having to expel you from school. Do you know that?"

Taïeb and Idriss were sitting on the floor, drawing at the coffee table. The TV was off. Djelila, Mom, and I were leaning our elbows on the dining table.

"Is this all because of your head scarf?" Mom asked.

"Yes, Mom."

"Then you have to remove it, Sohane. You have to remove this scarf. You'll have all the time you want to wear it later on. Lots of women wait until they get married. You know that."

"I'm not sure I want to get married, Mom," I answered, rolling my eyes, trying to lighten the mood. Djelila laughed.

"This is not funny!" Mom scolded us. "It's very serious. What will you do if they expel you, tell me?"

I sighed. "There are other ways, Mom. Correspondence courses, for instance."

I had thought about it all afternoon, in the library.

"What do you mean?"

"Long-distance teaching. You receive your courses by mail and you work from home—"

"Is it as good as real school?"

Mom stopped going to school when she finished tenth grade, after she had repeated it twice, if not three times. She's never talked much about that period of her life, only to tell us not to follow in her footsteps. "Education is your best friend, girls. Don't forget it," she always said.

"It's exactly the same," Djelila answered for me. "The only difference is that you don't see the teachers. You receive the courses by mail, you send them your homework, they grade it, and they send it back to you marked up."

"And you can get your diploma this way?"

I smiled. "Yes, Mom. I can get my diploma."

"Well, I don't know. Wouldn't it be simpler to continue at Racine?"

"They don't want me there anymore, Mom."

Dad came home at that moment. Right away he noticed that something was wrong: Djelila, Mom, and I were talking around the dining table, which seldom happened.

"What is going on?" he asked as he took off his jacket.

Mom shot me a look, which said it all: *You tell him. I don't have the courage.*

"I went to school with a head scarf this morning, and the teachers don't want me in their classes anymore," I explained. "They're talking about having me expelled."

Dad didn't seem to understand. "Your scarf?"

"Yes, I decided to cover my head," I told him.

Dad frowned. "So they want to expel you for that? You? One of their best students?"

Dad is unwavering in his beliefs that Djelila is the most beautiful girl on earth and that I'm the most intelligent one.

I sighed. "I'm not the best student at school, Dad."

"Are you telling me that they have a lot of students with grades as good as yours?"

"That's not the issue, Dad. They're talking about expelling me."

"Because you wore a scarf on your head? They can't kick you out because you cover your head, Sohane, it's impossible! Not because of a head scarf! What's wrong with your scarf, anyway?"

105

"They don't want any religious symbols in school. There's a law—and it includes head scarves."

"What business is it of theirs? You're not trying to convert your classmates to Islam, are you?"

I shook my head.

"So do they have a problem because you're Arab?"

"I'm not Arab, Dad. I'm French. And so are you!"

I had no idea how he would react to the situation, but his temper surprised me. Dad had never seemed compelled to follow the teachings of the Koran. He prayed, like Mom, like me, like Djelila. And until last year, he observed Ramadan, talked sometimes about making the pilgrimage to Mecca, and went to the mosque as often as possible, but he had never asked Mom to cover her head.

"Your uncle Ahmed is right," Dad muttered. "The French don't want us anymore. They were very happy to have us in the past to fill the ranks of their armies and to do cheap labor, but now they don't want our children."

Mom disappeared into the kitchen.

"They called a while ago to ask you and Mom to come to school tomorrow and meet with the school advisor and the principal."

"What for?"

"They want to explain why I'm not allowed to wear a head scarf in class, and they want you to convince me to take it off."

"Do you want to take it off?"

"No, Dad. I told them I don't intend to remove it."

"Then don't."

His support surprised me, but I tried not to show it.

"Is this what you want us to tell them tomorrow?" he asks me.

"Yes."

"Good."

Dad sat down. "Is dinner ready? I'm hungry."

That night, Djelila and I could hear our parents talking from our room. We could make out only snippets of conversation, but it was clear that Mom was trying to sway Dad. "If you tell her . . . you, she'll obey . . . the school . . . important . . . don't want to know . . . old enough to decide . . . they're not going to impose . . . if she wants to wear the head scarf, what right . . ."

We laughed and fell asleep.

The next morning, I got up at the same time as you, Djelila. I got dressed and you asked me why. "I'm going to study," I answered.

"If I were you I'd take a break."

I shook my head. "No, I'm going to register for correspondence classes today."

And that's what I did.

Dad came home earlier than usual to pick up Mom and they headed to Racine. He even changed into a suit, which made him look dapper and serious. When I told him what correspondence courses would cost, he took out his checkbook, filled in a check, and handed it to me.

Djelila came home shortly after that, looking flushed,

her hair all tangled. She threw her schoolbag down in the hall.

"What happened to you?" I asked.

"Guess!"

Seeing my astonishment, she filled me in.

"Majid and his lovely pals."

With everything going on, I had almost forgotten them.

"They hassled me again," Djelila said. "I'm fed up with those stupid punks. I'd like to slap their faces and send them crying to their mothers."

"I hope you didn't talk back to them," I said, suddenly worried by Djelila's anger.

"You bet I did! They called me a dirty slut and I don't know what else. I told them they were a bunch of impotent losers and they chased me until I reached our tower."

I must have looked pale as a ghost, because Djelila started laughing madly.

"Don't make such a face, Sohane. It's not true. I'm too scared of those guys to do that!"

"Stupid!"

"You got scared for me, So. Is that it?"

"Idiot. No, I got scared for them!"

"You know what's so stupid? Those guys bother me because I don't cover my hair and you're expelled from school because you want to cover yours. Isn't it ironic? By the way, I've got the latest gossip."

"What is it?"

"You have a support committee!"

"What?"

"Karine had the idea. We hatched a plan in the cafeteria during lunch. Everything is ready."

"What do you mean?"

"We wrote a petition demanding your unconditional readmission to school. We photocopied it and passed it around during recess."

"Karine?"

"Yes, and Estelle, Sylvan, Jerome, Basil, and some others. Here it is."

Djelila opened her bag and took out a sheet of paper with a paragraph scribbled in pen, complete with cuts, corrections, and additions in the margin. I was touched that they would do this for me even though I hardly knew them. They were Djelila's friends, not mine. We had never talked. Obviously, they knew I was Djelila's sister.

And they hadn't stopped at that.

Mom and Dad came back late from school. Djelila and I were feeding Taïeb and Idriss, who had become unruly. When I heard the key turn in the lock, my heart jumped hard and fast. Why? I wasn't expecting anything. No news they brought was going to change the decision I had made.

I had already decided that I would not go back to school, in spite of the petition and what followed later. I wasn't trying to draw attention to myself. I wasn't trying to provoke anyone. I simply was trying to find out who I was, not start a fight.

Actually, Dad and Mom didn't make any extraordinary

announcement. Dad sat and sighed while Mom took over with the little ones.

"So?" I asked. "What happened?"

"They want you to remove your head scarf," Dad said.

"What do you think?"

"I think you should do what you think is fair, Sohane." Dad's voice sounded harsh and tired at the same time. "Nobody has the right to ask you to deny your religion!"

I nodded. "Then I'll send my registration form for the correspondence classes tomorrow morning."

At school, Djelila and her friends' petition created some waves. I was the talk of Racine, along with my expulsion. The principal, the chief educational advisor, and some teachers organized a meeting with the students so that everyone could vent their feelings. Allowing people to be heard is a way to clean open wounds. Everyone expressed their opinions. Everyone but me, since I wasn't invited to the gathering. I was already banned from school.

In any case, nothing came of the meeting. Those who wanted to speak did, and it was acknowledged that head scarves could create a problem when worn in a public establishment. The teachers and principal gave speeches about safeguarding the country's democratic and secular principles. According to Djelila, Mrs. Desbeaux was very restrained. She spoke of freedom of religion and expression. . . . My sister also spoke. She tried to explain the paradox that shocked her: how I was required to remove my head scarf at school, while others in our housing projects wanted girls to be more traditional and conservative in their attire. But she only got limited responses, like "If you really agreed with your sister, you would wear the veil too" and "You support her because she's your sister."

Djelila kept me posted on the latest news. As for me, I kept studying. The truth is that the uproar didn't last long. The meeting took place two or three days after my departure. And then, slowly, everybody calmed down. Life went on: classes, homework, grades, parties. One week later, no one was talking about me.

News of Djelila took over.

News of Djelila's death.

Nineteen

I don't have any trouble adjusting to coursework through correspondence. I like it more than regular school. I like working alone and organizing my day the way I want. I can't say that I miss school. Sofia called me last night to offer her help. I told her I didn't need anything. Djelila asked if I was using my sudden freedom to take walks, watch TV, read. . . . No, not even that. It takes me a while to sort through the courses and write the essays. I've already gotten three of them back, graded: one in economics, one in English, and one in philosophy. The economics teacher congratulated me on my work. I got a good grade in English. And an A in French. I have some catching up to do, but I'm going to show everyone at Racine what's what. I don't need them to succeed. I'm going to graduate from high school no question!

Djelila has gone to basketball practice. She has a game tonight. She's not coming home first. Coach Abdellatif organized a pregame picnic in the gym. Each player is supposed to bring something to eat. Mom prepared a leek pie and a mushroom salad. Djelila was jumping like a flea with excitement when she left at two o'clock. "It's a very important game," she said. "The Montilan team has won all their games so far. If we can beat them, we'll end up leading in the tournament."

Of course, having permission to have dinner away from home adds to Djelila's fervor.

For some reason, though, I have an uneasy feeling about it.

Djelila told me that these past few days Majid and the others have been waiting for her every afternoon at school. Dressed in hoodies, they follow her to the projects, making sure to stay some ten steps behind her. They don't bother insulting her anymore. All they do is spit regularly in her direction. She's had it. She comes home in a worse state of nerves every evening. She's tried to focus on the upcoming game to avoid thinking about the constant stress of Majid. "When I play, I don't think about anything else. It's just the ball, our team, and the other team. I run, I pass, I push. The most important thing becomes the basket."

Djelila's eyes shine when she talks basketball.

They dim when she thinks about Majid and his gang of losers.

"What do they want?" she demands. "Why are they always on my back? What have I done to them?"

I don't answer. But I think her jeans are too tight—I gave her mine, finally—and her jacket is too short.

Djelila, my sweet Djelila, has become different lately, tougher, more aggressive, more of a soul in torment. My expulsion from school has rocked her. "How can outsiders give themselves the right to run our lives!" she rants.

I don't answer this either. I know that when she talks this way, she's thinking about Majid and his pals. Not about me.

I go back to the novel I'm reading, which I'll use for my next French essay. I love the book—it makes me think, and, normally, I wouldn't be able to put it down. But I can't concentrate on the story tonight. I can't stop thinking about Djelila.

The phone rings. Mom picks it up.

I come out of my room.

"OK, but not too late," Mom says. "I can trust you, right? You know that your father won't sleep until you get home. Yes, yes, dear. OK."

Mom hangs up.

"Was it Djelila?"

"Yes, the whole team wants to spend time together after the game. To celebrate if they win, commiserate if they lose."

"Is their coach going with them?" I ask.

Mom gives me a worried look. "I don't know."

"I'm sure he is," I reassure her. "He'll want to celebrate too."

"Probably," Mom agrees.

Unless he doesn't know about the outing. Unless the

girls "forgot" to invite him. In which case, there will likely be alcohol involved. And I suspect no one will have to beg Djelila to drink with them.

Djelila runs. Jumps. She is all arms and legs. She is everywhere on the court. Racine's opponents lead by two points. On the side, standing with his fists clenched, Coach Abdellatif shouts words of encouragement.

"Stay focused, Alice! Mark number five! Mark her!" he yells.

Djelila dribbles past one of her opponents. She has the ball. She is cornered; her thighs tense up, and, ultrafocused, she looks for an opening.

"Alice!" she shouts.

Alice dashes over just in time to catch the ball. Djelila is free. She runs to the basket. Alice understands and makes a long throw that Djelila catches. She makes a quarter turn, bends her knees, springs up on her legs, and jumps like a ballet dancer. The ball falls into the basket with a *whoosh*.

Alice and Djelila high-five quickly, and the game goes on. The girls from Montilan, in their orange jerseys, try to create an opening but don't succeed. Energized by Djelila's basket, her teammates don't give Montilan any room. Marine gets the ball, and with one pass, two passes, three passes, it's up to Djelila to throw again. The whole Montilan team is on her like bees on a honeypot. Djelila is hampered but traces an almost perfect curve, and the ball lands in the hoop.

The whistle blows. The game is over.

Djelila's teammates swarm around her, hug her, tousle her hair, and give her high fives.

I am cold. I snuggle as best I can in my jacket and keep my hands in my pockets. I've been here for ten minutes, but I didn't sit in the bleachers. I knew the game would end soon, so I decided to stand in the corridor, near the double doors.

After dinner, I watched TV with my parents at the same time that I played with Taïeb and Idriss. I couldn't keep still. I got up during a commercial and told my parents I was going to go root for Djelila and I would come back with her. Dad was all too happy to see me go. Mom gave me a grateful smile. They didn't want to say it, but they were clearly worried about Djelila as well.

My sister hasn't seen me.

Coach Abdellatif comes up to the girls and congratulates them. His smile shows off his pearly white teeth. His ponytail is undone. When the whistle signaled the end of the game, he removed the rubber band that tied his hair back and put it in his pocket. It was a gesture of victory, *his* victory gesture.

"Great job, girls! You played really well. Outstanding!" he tells them.

The girls from Montilan are already in the locker room. Their coach, a woman with short hair who's wearing an Adidas tracksuit, walks toward the Racine players.

"Brava, young ladies," she says with a smile. "It has been a real pleasure to play against you."

"Thank you," everyone says.

"Yeah, thank you. Your team played well too," Coach says.

Djelila, Alice, and the others try to look modest, but they don't quite succeed. Triumph is written all over their faces.

"Well, we have to catch our bus," the Montilan coach goes on. "I hope we'll have occasion to meet again. And next time we'll do what it takes to beat you. Believe me."

She shakes hands with Abdellatif, nods to the group, and leaves.

Abdellatif smiles from ear to ear. He waits until the woman has disappeared through the locker room door.

"We got them!" he shouts.

He beams like a kid. His eyes shine the way Taïeb's and Idriss's sparkle when Mom tells them a story.

Alice glances at Djelila, who nods imperceptibly. Alice clears her throat.

"Hey, Abdel, can we ask you something?" she says.

"Anything you want, Alice, anything!"

"Could you leave us the keys to the gym tonight? We'll drop them off in the morning, I promise."

Abdellatif frowns. "The keys to the gym? What for? You're not going to work out tonight, are you?"

Alice shrugs and smiles. "No, but we know that you've got to go and we'd all like to celebrate a little."

"Don't worry, girls," Coach says. "I've planned a celebration for next Saturday."

"But what about tonight?"

"Tonight, I can't. Sorry. I told you that I had to leave after the game."

"Yes, but can you leave us the keys?" Djelila tries.

Abdellatif shakes his head. "I can't do that, girls. I'm responsible for the gym, and if anything were to happen here—"

"But nothing will happen," Alice interrupts.

"I can't. Now go and change."

Alice opens her mouth to say something else, but Djelila touches her arm. No point insisting. Grumbling, the girls head toward the locker room. Djelila follows them. Alice follows Djelila, taking care to slouch her back and droop her shoulders so that Abdellatif feels guilty. As I watch the coach's face, I'd say she succeeded.

My sister still hasn't seen me.

No need to stay where I am. I step back and open one of the double doors. It is bitterly cold outside. A sharp wind freezes my nose. I rub my hands together. My head scarf protects my ears. In the parking lot, the Montilan team bus is waiting, its engine running. The exhaust pipe lets out a cloud of white smoke. The girls arrive one by one or in twos and threes. I can hear their coach near the locker room telling them to hurry. The only other vehicle in the parking lot is a green car. Abdellatif's car. A straggling girl, her bag on her shoulder, hurries out. The coach is right behind her. There's a hissing sound as the bus door closes, and the engine starts to run faster.

At the sound of voices, I turn my head. Djelila and Alice are the first Racine players to come out. They are laughing. Obviously Abdellatif's refusal to give them the gym keys hasn't upset them too much. I walk toward them.

"Sohane? What are you doing here?" Djelila says.

"I came to see you play," I tell her. "You were great."

"Really? You think so?"

The smile that lights up my sister's face is like a miracle.

"Yes, really."

Suddenly, Djelila frowns. "Did Dad and Mom ask you to come?"

"You know they're not like that. I came because I felt like it."

"I'm not going home right away."

"But . . . Abdellatif said that—"

"It doesn't matter," Alice declares, her eyes shining. "We're going to celebrate somewhere else!"

"Where?" I ask.

"We don't care! As long as we find a place to knock back our stash!"

Djelila nudges her friend. But it's pointless. I can guess that Alice is talking about alcohol.

"Djelila isn't going with you," I say. "She's coming with me."

Djelila gives me a look that could kill. "Hey, that's enough, Sohane. Who do you think you are? I go where I want, with who I want, and you can't order me around."

The biting wind has nothing to do with the feeling of

intense cold that invades my body. Girls stream out of the locker room. They glance over at us, wave to Djelila and Alice, and move on.

"Your teammates don't seem to be going to your little party," I say.

Alice shrugs. "Nobody else wants to come. 'It's too cold, it's too late, I have to go. . . .'" Alice adopts a baby voice to make fun of her teammates. "Lame. But Dje and I don't care! There are two of us, and that's enough."

More girls come out, chatting, followed by Abdellatif.

"Bye, girls. See you Tuesday for practice!" he says.

"Bye, Abdel, see you Tuesday," they answer.

He shuts the gym door carefully. Two turns of the key.

"Good night, Alice. Good night, Djelila. You should go home before you turn to ice."

"Yes, don't worry, we're going," Alice answers. "Bye."

"Bye."

Abdellatif climbs into his car. A few seconds go by. He turns the headlights on, starts the engine, backs up, blows the horn lightly, and he's gone.

"Good! Come, Dje, let's go," Alice says.

"Yeah, let's go."

"Djelila!"

"Get off my back, Sohane! It's time you realize I don't need a chaperone! I don't need you!"

"Djelila . . ."

Alice and Djelila walk off.

I hesitate. I'm tempted to follow them. I might still have

a chance to bring my sister back to reason. A giggle stops me short. The only thing is to go back home.

I walk fast. In my head, worry and irritation are waging battle. Djelila thinks she knows everything. She thinks she's cleverer than anyone else. She thinks she's behaving like an adult because she drinks alcohol. Good for her. But how can she do that to us? How can she do that to me? We are her family. Why does she need to reject us, to systematically go against everything we've been taught at home? She can't have forgotten the teachings of the Koran, God's demands. Tight jeans, cigarettes, and now alcohol. Do you hate us so much, Djelila? Are you ashamed of us? You disown your family, your culture, your education, your religion, you reject us, and you reject me. Why?

Quickly I make my way across the Lilac projects. Majid and his gang are leaning against the wall of Tower 38. As usual.

It would be better if they didn't see Djelila.

They might start in on her again. Would they dare hit her? Majid slapped her once, but I'm not sure he would be bold enough to strike her a second time. He's always been a coward. If he lays a hand on her again, it's likely he'll have to answer to Dad. But I'm sure they won't hesitate to shove her around. Which might teach her a lesson.

For all I care, she can go to hell!

In any case, I can't go home yet. Not without Djelila. Our parents wouldn't understand. And going to bed is out of the question: I wouldn't be able to sleep. I'm going to wait. And when she comes back, I'll give her a piece of my mind.

I sit on a bench, facing the patch of lawn that runs along our tower.

Anxiety is gnawing at me. What if Djelila doesn't come back? What if she decides to spend the whole night with Alice? What if something happens to them? I should have followed them to find out what they were up to. I glance at my watch. It's a quarter to eleven. Not very late. But when does she plan on coming back? When should I begin to worry? This is ridiculous since I'm already filled with dread.

I'm cold. I curl up a bit. I should have taken my gloves. My foot is moving by itself. I get up and walk around the square once, my eyes never leaving the door of our building to be sure not to miss her.

I pace up and down. The orange light of the streetlamp is flickering. Sometimes, when Djelila and I were little, we sat by our bedroom window and waited for all the project lights to go out. We couldn't do that today since the few working lights now remain lit all night.

Well, I have to stop thinking about Djelila. I'd be better off concentrating on the economics essay that I have to prepare for the end of next week. A really tough topic: *Once you have explained the reasons behind the adoption of a single currency in Europe, use the euro to demonstrate that a currency not only plays an economic role but should also be considered an institution.* I've analyzed all the correspondence lectures, all the documents supplied with the subject; I've reread my economics notes from before I left Racine High. And still I don't have a handle on it. But I have to get it done.

I look at my watch again. Eleven-fifteen. That's all! I can't believe it's only a quarter past eleven.

I go back to the bench and sit down. It's like sitting on an iceberg. I start hoping that Alice didn't take Djelila to friends of hers. A place where there are boys. Djelila is so pretty. . . . If she drinks alcohol . . . Why didn't I follow them? It was stupid of me. Maybe Djelila is in danger. She is so innocent!

What is certain is that when she comes back . . .

I get up again. I pace in front of the bench. A light goes off, then on, in a first-floor apartment of our tower. Maybe I should go back to the gym? No, I might miss her.

Eleven-twenty.

I no longer see Majid and the others. They probably split up, tired of trying to polish the dirty wall of Tower 38 with the backs of their jackets.

Djelila, Djelila. Where are you? What's going on in your head?

Her friend Alice has changed a lot. She started playing basketball at the same time as Djelila. She had braids then, and her mother used to bring her to basketball practice and pick her up afterward. Alice was pretty shy. Djelila thought she was silly, I remember. They didn't even talk to each other much.

I hear voices in the parking lot. Bursts of laughter.

Djelila.

I walk toward the blacktop alley to get a better view. It's her. She grabs onto Alice for support. Actually, they're shouldering each other to stay upright and laughing hysterically. They zigzag forward, stopping every two seconds to laugh again. Suddenly, Alice moves away, bends forward, her hands on her knees, and throws up. She wipes her mouth with a tissue, which she tosses on the ground. Djelila looks at her, startled at first, but Alice straightens up and they start laughing again. As if this is the funniest event of the year.

I think they're pathetic.

They hug and Alice moves off, unsteady on her feet.

I don't know where Alice lives and I couldn't care less. The stupid girl can walk across the whole projects by herself in twelve-degree weather if she feels like it. I don't give a hoot. I fold my arms. I'm going to tell Djelila exactly what I think.

As she stands alone in the middle of the parking lot, Djelila seems to hesitate. She looks around and raises an arm.

"Hey!" she says.

She can't have seen me.

She walks with determination, confidently, across the parking lot. She knows where she's going. I follow her gaze. Majid, Youssef, Brahim, Mohad, and Saïd have stopped. They are probably as surprised as I am. No way were they expecting to see Djelila stride toward them.

"Hey, Majid!" she says.

She stands in front of them, hands on her hips, defiant.

I am as still as a statue, not breathing. An alarm goes off in my head.

Get moving, Sohane, she's about to do something stupid. Do something. Go get her.

"So, you're not snug at home with your mom and dad?" Djelila says. Her voice carries across the empty parking lot. It sounds thick.

Majid mumbles something I can't hear. I know he spoke, because his head moved. His friends gather closer around, as if to protect him. To protect him from Djelila. What a joke!

"You know, I didn't appreciate what you did the other day," Djelila goes on. "Not at all, in fact. Slapping me like I'm a kid! And I always repay my debts!"

Time seems to have stopped. Majid doesn't have time to raise his arm to protect his face before Djelila raises her hand and deals him a massive slap. A humiliating slap. I start running over to them even before Djelila finishes talking. I am close to her. I grab her arm.

"Run, Dje! Run!"

She follows me. We run across the parking lot and the lawn that stands between us and the blacktop alley. We jump to the sidewalk and I drag her toward the door of our building. I don't dare look back. I pull her into the stairs. We run up the steps. Out of breath, I get the key out of my jacket, put it in the lock, and open the door. The hallway is silent. They didn't follow us.

I push Djelila in front of me and close the door.

She sits down on the floor and makes a funny sound in her throat.

I turn around. The idiot is laughing.

"Be quiet! You're going to wake up Dad and Mom," I warn her.

Djelila straightens, stretches her neck, and makes a ridiculous grimace.

"Yes, chief," she mumbles, before bursting into laughter again.

I feel like slapping her to bring her back to reality. Instead, I extend a hand. She looks at it a few seconds before grabbing it. I pull her up, ready to catch her if she's wobbly. But it's fine; she's steady.

"Thank you, Sohane," she whispers.

Her breath stinks of alcohol. I do not let go of her hand.

"Come."

"Girls?"

It's Mom.

"Is that you?"

"Yes, Mom, Djelila and I are back. She won her game."

"That's very good."

Our parents probably went to bed only a short while ago. I can see a ray of light under the door to their room.

"We're turning in, Mom. Djelila is dog-tired."

"Good. See you tomorrow."

If only Mom knew how tired Djelila is! If only Dad could see what his precious gazelle looks like tonight! Her hair tousled, her eyes vacant, a stupid smile on her lips.

In our room, Djelila falls onto her bed.

"Did you see how I laid into Majid! Did you see!" she says. "He didn't even have time to react."

I look at myself in the mirror and see that my head scarf is askew. A few pins must have fallen out. I begin to readjust it and then yank it off, angrily.

"You're crazy, Djelila, totally nuts!" I say.

Djelila sits up straight. "No, I'm not crazy. Majid deserved to be slapped, and twice more, if you ask me."

"Shut up, Djelila, you're getting on my nerves."

Djelila lies down again. "Oh, the ceiling is starting to spin," she says.

"Where were you tonight?"

"With Alice."

"Where?"

"Well, we didn't have any place to go, so we found a stairwell."

"A stairwell?"

I can't believe what I'm hearing. My sister behaved like a hobo!

"We didn't do anything wrong! We just wanted to have some fun. Did you see how well I played tonight?"

"What did you do in the stairwell?"

"Alice brought a bottle of whiskey."

"Do you drink like this often?" I ask, my voice sharper than a razor's edge.

"No, it's the first time."

"And why should I believe you?"

"Because it's the truth!"

"How many times have you drunk alcohol, Djelila?"

She doesn't answer right away. She looks for her pillow, props it up against the wall, and leans on it.

"Well?"

"I don't know. A few. I've had a drink with friends sometimes. . . . But I've never gotten drunk."

I feel exhausted, suddenly. I sit at my desk.

"You shouldn't drink, Djelila. You know that. You shouldn't. It's not a matter of religion or belief in God. It's bad. Anything could happen to you."

I look at her. Djelila shrugs.

"Promise me you won't do it again?"

"I don't know. I like to drink a little now and then, and I like to smoke a cigarette with my friends."

I hold back a sigh. "What did you drink tonight?" I finally ask.

"I told you. Whiskey."

"The whole bottle?"

Djelila nods.

"The whole bottle!"

"Alice drank more than I did," Djelila whispers. "Then she didn't feel well and it was getting late, so we decided to head home."

As if I hadn't noticed that Alice didn't feel well.

"Promise me you won't get drunk ever again, Djelila."

I'm not asking her never to drink alcohol, only not to drink too much. Djelila seems to understand the nuance. Right away she nods in agreement. At the same time I tell myself that I won't abandon her as I did. I won't abandon her again. I won't ditch you ever, Djelila.

"I was scared tonight," I say. "They could have—"

"If you're talking about Majid," Djelila interrupts me, folding her arms like a sulking child, "I don't regret anything. He got what he deserved!"

"But there were five of them and you were alone! They could have . . . I don't know. . . . You were at their mercy."

Djelila takes a deep breath before lifting her comforter. She removes her shoes with her feet and slips into the warmth of her bed.

"Aren't you getting undressed?" I ask.

"No, can't be bothered. Can you turn off the big light, please?"

Djelila turns over and brings the comforter up to her shoulders.

I turn on the bedside lamp, shut off the ceiling light, and start taking off my shoes. My sister is still.

"You OK, Djelila?"

"Hmm."

I take off my socks, jeans, and sweater, put on a large T-shirt, and remove my bra from under the T-shirt. My anger is gone. All I can see is the top of Djelila's head. I feel like going over to stroke her hair. I feel like taking her in my arms and rocking her like a baby. I close my eyes instead.

"Sohane . . ."

I open my eyes. My sister has not moved. Her voice is muffled through the thickness of the down comforter.

"You're wrong, Sohane," Djelila says.

"Wrong about what?"

"I don't want to be afraid of Majid or anyone else. I don't want to live in fear. I don't want my choices to be dictated by fear. I don't want to be what others have decided I should be. I want to be myself. Do you understand, Sohane?"

I come up with only one answer. "It's not a reason to drink," I say.

Djelila shrugs slightly under the covers.

"Sleep well, Djelila."

"Thanks. You too, Sohane."

Djelila doesn't utter a word to me all Sunday. She does her best to stay far away from me. She gets up late and takes a long shower. She hardly touches her breakfast, and then she helps Mom prepare lunch. She has brushed her hair, and it shines in the sunlight that floods the kitchen. She doesn't seem particularly tired, and she welcomes Dad's congratulations with a smile.

"So you beat them, you won your game? Brava, Djelila, brava!"

"Thanks, Dad."

She brings him his coffee, and he's happy to have his darling daughter take such good care of him. She takes Taïeb and Idriss for a walk, helps them finish their homework, and gives them a bath.

She seems to be elsewhere.

131

She goes to bed early. When I come in, she pretends to be asleep.

Monday morning, she leaves for school without even saying goodbye, and when she comes home, she dives into her homework.

The phone rings and Mom calls her. I'll bet anything it's Alice. Djelila stays on the phone a long while without talking much. Eventually I walk out to the corridor as if I'm going to the bathroom. Djelila quickly turns to face the wall.

She hangs up and tells Mom that the next day's basketball practice is canceled. "Abdellatif is sick," she says.

Tuesday, she leaves without talking to me.

I keep thinking about her all day—which explains why I don't finish the outline of my economics essay on the euro.

It's a nice day. The sun shines on the square, almost giving it an air of cheerfulness in spite of the dog poop and dirty papers littering it. I look at the books that are open on my desk. Suddenly I'm tired of constantly studying. I need some fresh air. I look at my watch. Djelila should be back soon. I put my head scarf on, adjust it with pins, and slip my jacket on.

"Mom, I'm going out for a walk," I say. "Do you need anything?"

"No, dear," Mom answers from the kitchen, where she's giving Taïeb and Idriss their afternoon snack.

I open the front door and shut it behind me.

I hear a dog barking. A dog howling.

But it is not a dog.

I run down the stairs. All the way down.

The howling is coming from the basement. I push open the door and rush in. All I can see are flames—flames and your body twisting. I hear your screams and see your body collapse. I see Majid and your burnt body. Everything else I register without really seeing—the matches, the dirty green can. I am on top of Majid and I hit him. I hit him with all my might. My fists clenched, I hit his face, his eyes, his mouth, and I howl. I howl too.

Twenty

Howling. This need to howl is still in the pit of my stomach. To howl with fury and pain.

I'm glancing at an article about my sister's death. I couldn't bring myself to read any of them, but I bought all the newspapers. I kept them without ever looking at them. I've taken this one out of the drawer almost involuntarily. On one side is a picture of Djelila, the familiar school ID picture; on the other side is a picture of Majid at the time of his arrest. I do not remember any of it. The picture is blurry, the frame small. His hoodie covers his head, so it's difficult to make out his face. He is handcuffed. A man, a police officer probably, is holding his arm.

The article mentions a phrase that the police—without any doubt—fed to the journalists following the murderer's first questioning: *"I swear on my mother's head, I wanted to teach her a lesson, so I had to do something big."*

My eyes scan the first lines of the article.

> *A sixteen-year-old girl died yesterday, burnt alive in the basement of the Lilac housing projects.*
> *The alleged murderer, a minor who knew the victim and lived a few buildings away from her, offered no resistance and has been arrested. Paramedics and emergency room doctors could do nothing to save the victim.*
> *Everyone in the Lilac projects demands justice. . . .*

"Dead." "Burnt alive." "The victim."

All these words are about my sister, Djelila.

For nearly a year now, I have retreated to my room. I come out only to eat and run some errands at hours when the projects are empty. For nearly a year I have created this jail to punish myself for not saving you. I have created this refuge so I won't have to think that you are no longer here—and that you will never be coming back. Never. I thought about running away. I wanted to forget you, to stop the pain. But it isn't that easy. Wherever I go, whatever I do, your memory haunts me. Djelila.

Today a ray of sunshine comes through my bedroom window, *our* bedroom window, and floods your comforter. Just like on the day you died. Yes, there was a day when you died. That day exists. You are dead. I close my eyes, trying to forget, but I cannot.

This morning a letter came for me in the mail. I put it on my desk without paying attention to it. Now I push the newspaper back and open the envelope. It is a letter to all seniors enrolled in correspondence courses, reminding us to register for the final-year exam. The exam I was unable to face after your death and put off for a year.

No use trying to work any more today. I am in no mood to understand what I'm reading; my mind is simmering with fears, doubts, and anger. I grab my head scarf from the back of my chair and adjust it on my head with motions that have become familiar to me. I put my jacket on, take my bag, and go out without a glance at my work.

At the foot of our tower, I stop for the first time in front of the stone slab embedded in the ground. My sister's name is engraved on it. I've always refused to stop and look at it. I know that it had to be cleaned two or three times, when red spray paint was used to sully it with slurs like BITCH and WHORE. I don't know who took care of the cleanup. Djelila's friends, maybe. That's definitely possible.

This slab is only a slab. Djelila's body is at the cemetery. Buried with an unmarked headstone. And Dad pretends your soul is in Algeria. You, who were so French. Maybe he's right.

The tags that drip down the facade of Tower 38 have not been painted over, but since Majid's arrest, neither Brahim nor Youssef, nor anyone else, hangs out there.

Today is Wednesday. Children are playing in the square. I can hear their shouts and their laughter. I imagine mothers seated on the benches, watching them. Taïeb and Idriss are at an after-school program.

I walk across the projects. I have not boarded a bus for ages.

I walk slowly, letting the sun warm my cheeks. It's a pleasant feeling. Do I have the right to enjoy this warmth knowing you are dead and will never feel anything again? I inhale deeply. The air smells of dust and exhaust fumes. Just like always.

What I see first is your name. It's written in bold letters on a small poster taped to a streetlamp pole. DJELILA. I stop without thinking and read:

FOR YOU, DJELILA

Wednesday, November 15, at 2.30 p.m.,
at the Community Center, 25, rue du Portugal
Discussion about the death of Djelila Chebli
Victim of violence in projects
Numerous people will talk

My watch says it's ten past three. The community center is two steps away, at the end of the blacktop alley. I can see the building, its metallic structure adorned with glass. Modern and sleek. There is no hurry for me to register for exams. I can do that tomorrow or even next week.

I don't know if it's curiosity, the desire to hear people talk about my sister, or an unhealthy motivation that pushes me in the direction of the center, but I am soon in front of its main door.

I open it. In the hall, a woman behind a desk is writing in a large notebook. I go up to her.

"Excuse me."

The woman raises her head.

"I'm looking for the room where the discussion about Djelila Chebli is taking place," I tell her.

"In the corridor. The first one. The blue door on your right."

"Thank you."

"But it started a while ago."

I do not reply. I make my way to the room and knock on the door. No answer. I can hear a woman's voice.

I walk in noiselessly. Fortunately, the door opens at the rear of the room, so I'm not too conspicuous. A few faces turn to observe me. Some twenty people are seated in rows of chairs. There are only two men—no, three. I sit down. A woman turns toward me, then leans to her neighbor and whispers a few words in her ear. The other woman looks at me too. I try not to pay attention. Behind a large table, a short-haired woman speaks into a microphone. I don't understand what she's saying. It's not that she doesn't speak clearly, but I have a hard time concentrating. I distinguish words like "sociologist," "uneasiness in the suburbs," and "rise of Islam." I need to scratch my neck. I feel like I'm sweating and yet it's pretty cold in the room.

I breathe slowly and try to focus on the words of the speaker.

People in the first row become agitated. There are whispers. Up at the microphone, the sociologist stops speaking.

A tall woman gets up and comes toward me.

Does she recognize me? Is she going to ask me to talk and give my opinion on the tragedy? No, it's not possible that anyone knows who I am. How could they recognize me? Was there ever a picture of me in the newspaper at the time of the funeral?

Panic takes hold of me. I can't. I don't want to. And then . . .

The woman leans toward me.

"Young lady?"

"Yes."

"We would like you to leave."

I look straight at her. My panic is gone. Why is she asking me to leave?

"You don't belong here. Our group fights for the liberty of women, for the defense of their free will, and for the abolition of a chauvinist society. You disavow these values by accepting to wear the veil."

I feel like shouting, not out of pain this time, but out of amusement at the irony. Of course, how did I forget? I can't participate in a debate that uses my sister as a symbol! I probably can't even be Djelila Chebli's sister, not the Djelila Chebli these women have chosen as the mascot for their own convictions!

It doesn't matter. I get up, and without saying a word, I leave. I cross the hallway, almost running. I need fresh air.

A crushing fatigue invades me. I feel more exhausted than if I had run a marathon.

Twenty - One

"Sohane, Sohane."

I wake up with a start. My tangled hair falls on my face. Idriss's eyes are fixed on mine. I need a few seconds to find my bearings. The community center, the meeting . . . yes, that's right, and I came back home. Right away. I did not register for the exam. I will do it tomorrow. I was so tired. I lay down on Djelila's bed and must have fallen asleep like a log. The clock reads 7:30.

"It's almost dinnertime, Sohane," Idriss says.

I smile at him. He seems to have forgotten the Do Not Enter rule. He has round and rosy cheeks, dusky skin, curly hair that falls to his neck, and large dark eyes in which you can read his concern.

I sit up.

I haven't looked at my little brother for a long time.

He hesitates a moment and puts his hand over mine. I shiver.

"You know," he whispers, "I miss her too."

I nod. My throat is so tight that I cannot speak.

"I know you're sad," my brother goes on. "I'm sad too."

"Yes, Idriss, I know you're sad."

"Do you know what else makes me sad?"

I shake my head.

"Ever since Djelila died, you're never here either."

Died. He can say it, this word, my little brother.

"I'm not gone, Idriss. I'm always home."

"It's like you are gone."

How could I forget? How could I forget them—Idriss, Taïeb, Dad, and Mom?

Idriss holds my hand tight.

"I get the message, Idriss. I'll be back."

"You know, I can write pretty well now."

Twenty - Two

After dinner, I take the telephone directory. I remember Karine's family name, Bilassovitch. A name so uncommon it's easy to find.

I call her. She doesn't seem surprised when I introduce myself. I tell her that I've thought about the suggestion that she, Estelle, Sylvan, and the others have for the memorial of Djelila's death. My voice hardly chokes when I pronounce this last word.

"Thank you, Sohane," Karine says. "Thank you from all of us. Should we meet to talk about it?"

"OK."

"At the Green Handkerchief, after school tomorrow?"

At the Green Hanky.

"Sure. At the Green Handkerchief tomorrow around five."

"See you then, Sohane."

* * *

The following day, for the first time in a long while, I go to pick up Taïeb and Idriss at school. I prepare them lunch—chicken cutlets and mashed potatoes. Nothing gourmet, but I think they like it. They talk nonstop about the teachers, their friends. . . . If I understand correctly, Taïeb had a problem over marbles during recess and Idriss came to his rescue. When I take them back to school, Idriss runs toward his friends, but Taïeb sticks his cheek against mine, kisses me, and whispers in my ear, "See you later, Sohane."

I spend the afternoon watching my clock. At four, I'm ready to go, feeling equally impatient and anxious.

I sit at the back of the Green Handkerchief, at a table where I can see the door, and I wait.

It's only when I see them come in together that I manage to acknowledge what has taken so long to evolve in my mind, the knowledge that I had so much trouble accepting: I was wrong, Djelila. Your jeans were not too tight, and your jacket was not too short. You had the right to be yourself. But others decided otherwise. I forgot the principles of the Koran. I should not have judged you, Djelila. I should have been more understanding. In any case, I should have defended you. I did not relate to your rebellion, but it was a mistake, Djelila. You were right. Freedom is everything.

Karine is the first to sit next to me.

"Thank you, Sohane," she says, looking at me. "Thank you for coming."

144

Twenty-Three

We walk slowly, heads down. We hold the banner that stretches across the whole street: WE HAVE NOT FORGOTTEN YOU, DJELILA!

These are the words we chose.

Dad and Mom follow the procession with Taïeb, Idriss, and Hana Leïla. Many of Djelila's school friends are here too, along with Coach Abdellatif and all of Djelila's teammates. Alice is crying when I see her. Little by little, many others join the march. Men, women—some of them veiled, some not—young girls, pretty and wearing makeup, their hair falling down their backs, many different ethnicities.

No one wants to forget Djelila.

We stop in front of the tower, the one where I still live

today. Behind us, Estelle carries a huge bouquet of flowers. She kneels down to lay it on top of the slab.

It was a year ago. One year exactly.

My eyes fill with tears. Finally I give myself permission to say goodbye to you, Djelila. I will try to keep my fears at bay; I will try to think that you will always be with me.

I did not cover my head this morning. It was useless. My head scarf is not a pronouncement. I do not want it to be used as justification for any kind of violence.

Karine lets go of the banner to join Estelle in front of the slab. She holds a piece of paper in her hand. A short text that we wrote together.

Her voice is shaking.

"We are gathered here to remember the victim of a terrible crime—Djelila Chebli. It is for Djelila that we cry today. She is not a symbol of a broken youth and even less the symbol of a divide between two cultures. Djelila was none of that. All Djelila wanted was to live, that is all. We are here for our sister, the sister we will not forget, our sister, Djelila."

My cheeks are covered with tears. I cry at last.

AUTHOR'S NOTE

Up until 1989, in France, the right of Muslim girls to wear head scarves in public schools was not often considered. But as principals and education boards began to complain that broadcasting one's religion in a secular establishment was at odds with a public institution of learning, girls who chose to cover their heads began to be suspended, even expelled. A prominent 1989 case—known as *L'Affaire du Foulard* ("The Headscarf Affair")—involving three Muslim girls, all banned from the same school for wearing head coverings, spotlighted the controversy. Similar cases followed. Many educators began pushing for a legal ruling. Soon the debate grew heated, feeding the headlines.

On March 15, 2004, the French government passed a law prohibiting public school students from wearing any conspicuous religious symbols or religious attire. This includes head scarves.

In writing *I Love I Hate I Miss My Sister*, I have not intended to tackle the question of whether head scarves should be permitted in schools, but I very much want to raise questions regarding the freedom of women and their right to choose how to live their lives. The novel was inspired by a true and horrifying event that galvanized the attention of all of France in 2002—the death of Sohane Benziane, a seventeen-year-old French girl of Algerian descent, who was murdered. Sohane Benziane was doused with gasoline and burnt alive by Jamal Derrar, a boy who was said to be settling a score with Sohane's boyfriend. Derrar and his accomplice, Tony Rocca, were sentenced to twenty-five and eight years of prison time, respectively.

I hope *I Love I Hate I Miss My Sister* sparks conversations about civil liberties for girls and women—and the ways we can fight to prevent violence against women globally.

GLOSSARY

Algeria: A country in North Africa, located between Morocco and Tunisia, on the Mediterranean coast. Its capital is Algiers, and the official language is Arabic. From 1830 to 1962, Algeria was a French colony, which is why there are many Algerian immigrants in France and why many French are of Algerian descent.

Allah: Arabic for "God."

babouche: A heelless slipper that comes in a wide variety of colors, usually made of leather with embroidery and/or other decorative flourishes.

burka: A full-body cloak worn by Muslim women.

darbuka: A single-membrane drum with a goblet-shaped body, larger at the top and tapered toward the bottom. The instrument is used mostly in the Middle East, North Africa, and Eastern Europe.

djellaba: A loose-fitting robe with a pointy hood that is worn by men and women, especially in Morocco, but also in all North African countries where Arabic is spoken. The garment is made of cotton for summer and wool for winter.

hamdullah: Arabic for "praise to Allah," this expression is often said after finishing a meal.

hana: Arabic for "grandmother."

hijab: A head scarf worn by Muslim women when in the presence of men unrelated to them. It typically covers the forehead, hair, and neck, though many variations exist. Sometimes the entire face is hidden, with only the eyes visible.

imam: The prayer leader in a mosque, always a man.

inshallah: Arabic for "God willing."

Islam: A monotheistic religion that follows the teachings of the Koran.

jadi: Arabic for "grandfather."

Koran: The main religious text of Islam, believed by Muslims to be the actual word of Allah.

Mecca: Located in the Middle East country of Saudi Arabia, Mecca is considered the holiest city in the Islamic religion. It is the birthplace of Mohammed, the prophet to whom the Koran was revealed. Muslims try to make at least one pilgrimage (known as the Hajj) to Mecca in their lifetime.

Mohammed: Considered the last prophet of Allah in the Islamic religion.

muezzin: The person who leads the call to prayer in a mosque.

Muslim: A person whose religious faith is Islam.

Ramadan: The ninth month of the Islamic calendar is observed worldwide as a month of fasting. From dawn to sunset, Muslims refrain from consuming food, drinking liquids, smoking, and sexual relations, and, in some interpretations of the Koran, from swearing.

Salaam alaikum: An Arabic greeting used by Muslims worldwide. Roughly translated, it means "Peace be with you"— used as the equivalent of "hello" or "good day" in English.

surah: A chapter of the Koran, of which there are 114.

tagine: A traditional dish of North Africa—a stew of meat and vegetables—slow-cooked in a special dome-shaped earthen pot from which the dish takes its name.

youyou: A cadenced, piercing cry emitted by Muslim women during special ceremonies such as weddings and funerals.